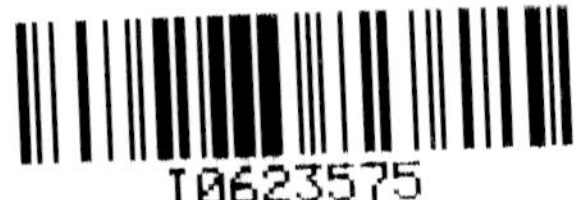

Schoolhouse Justice

Heartland Heartstoppers, Book 1

By Helen Gray

Written by: Helen Gray
Published by: Forget Me Not Romances, a division of Winged Publications

ISBN-13: 978-1-946939-71-5
ISBN-10: 1-946939-71-4

Author Note

Schoolhouse Justice is book one of a new, in progress trilogy titled **Heartland Heartstoppers** that is a spinoff of an earlier series, **Heartland Heartmates**. The difference in the two series is that Heartmates is a romance series, but Heartstoppers is a romantic mystery series. It is my hope that readers will enjoy both.

When justice is done, it brings joy to the righteous but terror to evildoers.

Proverbs 21:15 (NIV)

Chapter 1

Lanell Rhodes patrolled the sidewalk in front of Central High School, her gaze scanning the parking lot not yet filled with buses and personal vehicles. She walked at a brisk pace, trying to keep warm in the Monday morning after Thanksgiving blustery cold. She always arrived well ahead of the staff and students. Within a few more minutes teachers, and then buses and students driving cars, would begin pulling into the parking lot.

As the school's resource officer, one of her duties was to monitor their arrivals and departures. She was also expected to provide law enforcement services to the school, be sure everything and everyone was kept safe, investigate allegations of illegal incidents and refer students to juvenile authorities when necessary. She interacted with the students, provided lockdown drills and security training, attended their extracurricular and athletic events, investigated transportation complaints, and made arrests when necessary. She had no trouble staying busy.

Seeing nothing out of order, she looped around at

the end of the building and returned to the main entrance, thinking longingly of a hot cup of coffee from the teachers' lounge. She pulled the door open and stepped inside the front lobby.

The sight of Dale Whitaker, the girls' softball coach and physical education teacher, pushing a wheeled cart down the locker-lined hall was an ordinary sight. What wasn't ordinary was the overly heavy load of items weighing down her cart, several of which suddenly went sliding off the pile and clattered onto the concrete floor.

Lanell dashed to Dale's side. "Let me help you," she said, stooping to gather what looked to be small tools and decoration supplies used in constructing booths and games for the past Friday night's fundraiser that the athletic department had conducted to purchase Christmas gifts for needy children. Together they placed everything back on the cart.

"Where are you headed?" Lanell asked.

Dale, an attractive, dark-haired woman in her late thirties, grinned. "I had hoped to get these borrowed materials back to the shop before classes start."

"Let's go." Lanell pushed, and together they rolled the overloaded cart on down the hallway and out the door. When they arrived at the outer entrance to the industrial arts department, they found the main door closed, indicating no teachers had entered yet, even though Vernon Ziegler's pickup was parked near the building.

Lanell reached for the door handle and pushed, not expecting it to open. But it did. She stepped forward and peered inside the silent room that reeked of sawdust, oil, and an eerie sense of something not being right. She pushed the door opening wider and edged into the room, glancing around quickly. Morning light filtered through the windows, showing work tables with small, hand-held tools on them. But the benches were empty of the hydraulic and power tools that normally occupied them. The hairs on the back of Lanell's neck prickled.

Her hand went to the back of her duty belt and grasped the handle of her weapon. She pulled it forward and advanced farther into the room, sweeping her gaze about the perimeter of the huge area. As her head turned to glance back over her shoulder, her breath caught. She rushed to the side of the man lying prone on the floor next to the wall where the door had swung back and partially concealed him. She dropped to her knees beside him.

A gasp from Dale made Lanell glance up at the teacher's ashen face. "Go get your principal," she ordered, while placing a finger on the man's neck to check for a pulse. "I'll call my department." She worked for the local police department, but this school was her permanent assignment throughout the term.

"What's wrong?" Dale asked faintly, frozen in place.

Lanell pulled her hand from the prone teacher's neck and reached for her phone. "He's dead. And it looks like the place has been looted."

Dale gasped again, whirled, and ran to do as instructed.

While calling in the report, Lanell visually examined Vernon's body. Blood had oozed into a dark pool on the floor and dried around the edges. A bloody hammer lying about a foot away from the man's shoulder had to be the weapon used to bash in the poor teacher's head.

Within minutes the shrill sound of sirens reached her from a distance. The police arrived moments later, and an ambulance wasn't far behind. Soon the room was populated with paramedics and a pair of officers. Then the high school principal, Blake Autry, rushed into the room. He looked at the body, and wrenched his head away, obviously shaken.

Moments later Detective Evan White, a middle aged man wearing a dark suit, joined them and went directly to the victim. After confirming that the man was dead, he faced the principal. "Lock down the school immediately."

Mr. Autry nodded and pulled out his phone.

"You found the body?" Evan asked Lanell.

She nodded. "A teacher and I were returning a cart loaded with items she had borrowed from Vernon last week. I sent her to notify the principal while I called you guys."

He pulled out his notebook. "What's her name? You know I'll need to talk to her."

"Dale Whitaker. She teaches physical education and coaches the girls' softball team." She went on to explain in more detail how they had come to be there together.

"The school is being locked down," the principal reported, his voice strained. "I need to get back to my office and oversee everything."

The detective nodded. "Keep everyone in the gym. We'll let you know when it's okay to continue with your normal schedule." He grimaced as he said the word normal.

"If we can keep everyone until noon and be able to count the day, I think we should send them home after that," the principal said. "When they find out what's happened, the students and staff are bound to be too upset to continue classes."

"That sounds like a plan," Evan said. "Go take care of business, and ask the staff to meet somewhere after the students have been sent home. It might reassure them a little if I give them a brief report."

"Thanks." Blake turned and left.

The next hour was spent in solemn work. The crime scene was secured, assessed, processed, and documented. To be thorough, they included the entire room and the area outside the building around and including where Vernon's truck was parked. Then the evidence technicians went to work with their cameras and measuring devices, determining distance, angles, and trajectories, and searched for trace evidence that might prove helpful later.

Lanell did a walk-through of the facility with Evan. "It looks like Vernon walked in on a burglary," she said as he checked the windows.

He nodded and stepped away from the one that was broken. "It appears that thieves—I don't think this was a solo job—entered, and then broke this window. The fragments of glass outside it tell me it was broken from the inside. So someone apparently had a key, entered through the doorway, and broke out the window to make us think that's how they got inside the place. They must have had a truck parked outside and loaded whatever power tools and equipment they were stealing from here onto it."

The impact of his words hit Lanell square in the

face. "So there's an accomplice, someone on the inside who has, or can get, access to room keys."

"That's how it looks."

"In that case, this person must also be feeding them information about what to take and where to find it."

His response was a grim-faced nod. "I've sent the principal a message to have his other shop teacher—he said there are two—make a list of exactly what all is missing."

"Vernon's pickup is parked outside," Lanell noted. "And there are some building supplies and lumber in the back of it. He must have been delivering materials he planned to use in class this week, and was jumped as he entered."

"It looks that way. The thieves never expected a teacher to show up late on a Sunday night."

His words made Lanell shake her head. "Vernon's arrival panicked them, and somebody grabbed the first thing handy—that hammer." She tipped her head toward the bloody weapon still lying on the floor. "He hid behind the door and jumped Vernon from behind."

"It was a weapon of convenience," Evan agreed. "The scenario seems fairly clear, except for one thing. Why did Vernon walk in on them? He should have seen their vehicle outside."

"He must have recognized it and thought there was a logical reason for it being there," Lanell said, glancing at her watch.

Evan read the action. "Go on back to your duties. I'll see that everything is wrapped up here. Then I'll talk to the superintendent and principal and tell them what we've determined—or as much as I can. Then I'll talk to Mrs. Whitaker—with you present."

Lanell nodded. "I'll check on Dale. I think she's a strong type, but I want to be sure she's not too shaken up over this. I'll let her know to expect you."

~

Connor Prescott steered his white Yukon SUV into the parking lot of the high school, his gut tight with concern. His boss, Justin Whitaker, had contacted him from out of state and said someone in his Springfield office had reported to him that there had been a murder here at Central High School, and his wife's name had been mentioned as some kind of witness.

Before her marriage, softball Coach Dale Denning had gone beyond normal bounds to help Connor and his younger sister when their mother died. Miss Denning had taken them into her home after their mother's funeral and kept them there while she and a work crew from her church repaired their parents' deteriorated little house and made it possible for them to live in it independently, stay in Springfield, and finish high school there. After graduation, Connor had attended college locally at Missouri State University while Carly finished high school, and then done a stint in the Air Force and become a pilot. When he discharged, Justin Whitaker had offered him a job at his charter airline service as their safety officer. In addition to those duties, he piloted some charter flights.

He and Carly owed their former teacher more than they could ever repay. So if Dale was in any kind of trouble, her husband knew Connor would do anything he possibly could to help.

Near the front entrance he spied a female police officer, strutting her authority in her dark blue uniform, regulation coat, and gloves. The duty belt around her waist was loaded with enough gear—handcuffs, gun, magazine clip, mace, Taser, flashlight, baton, radio, phone—to weigh her down.

He zipped his coat to his chin and stepped out into the wind that had built to a blast. A few flakes of snow were beginning to whirl about. As he approached the officer, he noted that she wasn't real tall, maybe five-foot-four or five inches, but her erect body carriage made her seem taller. Honey-blond hair wreathed her face and sculpted about her head. When she spotted him, she immediately veered toward him.

"No one is allowed inside, Sir." Her tone was firm.

"I need to check on the well-being of my boss's wife," he said just as firmly.

Her head moved back and forth. "No one can enter now."

"Can you tell me if Miss Denning …I mean Mrs. Whitaker is okay? Her husband said he heard she was present when a murdered teacher was found."

The officer's brow creased. "You're related to Dale?"

"No, she was my sister's softball coach, and she …looked after us when our mother died. So she's more of a mother figure to us. Is she okay?"

The officer studied him, her stiff spine and body language telling him she wasn't giving an inch. But then she softened just a bit. "Classes will be dismissing right after lunch, which will be in a few minutes," she finally said. "As soon as they're gone, the teachers are to meet in the library. If you'll wait outside, or leave and return in about an hour, I can tell Dale to come meet you after the staff assembly adjourns. What's your name?"

The square set of her shoulders told him she wasn't going to change her stance and allow him entrance. Considering the severity of what had happened, he understood. It still irritated him, but he knew when he was beaten.

"Just tell her Connor is here. I'll be back in an hour."

And he was. After driving into town and getting a burger and fries at a fast food drive-through, he returned to the parking lot and ate in his vehicle where he could keep an eye on the entrance.

When students began pouring from the building, he waited for the buses to load and leave. Then he approached the entrance again. The officer was not there, but he spotted her through the glass panes beside the doors. She stood at the entrance to the library, located at the left, facing the principal's office across the lobby.

When he opened the door, she turned and saw him. Lips tightening, she strode to meet him. "I said I would let her know you're here. She hasn't arrived yet."

As she finished the statement, Connor caught sight of Dale coming down the hallway toward them. She spied him at the same time and picked up her pace.

Before the officer was aware of her presence, Dale grabbed Connor and hugged him. "You didn't need to come, but I'm happy to see you," she said when she released him.

He gripped her hand. "Justin called me from Canada. He didn't order me to come, but I know he wants a first-hand report. He said something happened to Vernon."

Dale nodded in short, jerky motions, tears filling

her eyes. "Lanell and I took a cart of stuff to the shop and found him." Her voice was unsteady.

The resource officer nudged her arm. "The meeting is starting."

"I have to go," Dale said, moving away. "Will you come to supper this evening?"

"Justin already asked us."

As she disappeared into the library, the officer faced him, her expression questioning. "Is there a personal connection between Dale and the victim?"

Connor swallowed, struggling to regain his momentarily lost composure. "Vernon is …was another of her pass-it-on projects."

When she frowned, he indicated the library door with a head motion. "Do you have to be in there with the staff during their meeting?"

"I need to be close," she said, speaking quietly. "We can stand here during the meeting, and I'll peek inside every few minutes. Tell me what you mean by pass-it-on project."

They stepped over near the wall. "When Dale and her twin brother were kids, they were abandoned by their mother and taken in by a kind neighbor lady. The woman told them the way they could repay her was to pass the kindness on to others any time opportunities came along. Dale did that for Carly and me. We weren't the first—or the last. Vernon's parents split during his senior year, and he stayed with Dale and Justin until he graduated."

~

Lanell kept her face carefully expressionless, having almost blurted something when Connor stated his sister's name. She scrutinized his features, studying each detail. Yes, she could see the resemblance now. She hadn't known of Carly's relationship with Dale Whitaker.

Suddenly the library door opened, and staff members began to emerge. The meeting had been briefer than she had anticipated. When Dale exited, Detective White was at her side. When he spotted Lanell and Connor, he gripped Dale's arm and steered her to a halt beside them.

"Can you join us in the gym?" he asked Lanell.

She glanced around. The principal was entering his office. "I'll tell Mr. Autry where I'll be."

"I'd like Connor with us," Dale said.

Lanell locked gazes with the detective, expecting his refusal to allow a non-involved person to sit in on their discussion.

"I need his moral support," Dale insisted, pressing the issue.

Evan ran a measuring glance over him. "I suppose it'll be all right."

Lanell dashed across the lobby to the principal's office. He had entered his private domain and was sinking into his chair when she stepped inside the doorway. "If you need me, I'll be in the gym with the detective and Mrs. Whitaker." She didn't mention Connor.

He nodded wearily, raking a hand through his hair. "Thanks."

She caught up with the trio at the gym door. Inside, Evan led the way to a spot on the bottom bleacher and stood facing it. He indicated they should sit. "I need formal statements from you two who found the body."

Lanell noted how Dale's hand gripped Connor's as

she fought tears.

Evan cleared his throat and addressed Lanell. "You and Mrs. Whitaker were the only ones present when you found Mr. Ziegler. Is that right?"

Lanell nodded. "Yes, it is."

"Who saw him first?"

"I did."

"Why were you there?" He aimed the question at Dale, but spoke in a softer tone when he read the grief in her expression. "Just take your time and tell me everything you did this morning."

Dale took a deep breath and gave him a step by step account of what she had done and seen.

"The door wasn't locked?" he asked when she finished.

"That didn't surprise me," Lanell answered. "The teacher's truck was parked near the door, so we assumed he was around somewhere."

"I'm sure you've both formed opinions about what happened. Care to share them with me?" He looked from one to the other of them.

"It looked like equipment was missing," Dale said. "So I'm guessing it was another robbery."

He frowned. "Another?"

Lanell knew he was aware of what Dale meant, but he was looking for insights and impressions. There had always been burglaries in the city, but it seemed like a crime wave had struck in the past three or four months.

"Not long after school started, batteries were stolen from the buses," Dale said.

Suspects had cut holes in the fence that enclosed the bus lot and climbed through to the bus barn. They had popped open the two side panels of twelve buses, cut the wires connected to the batteries, and stolen both batteries from each bus. Most likely they had been sold to recycling centers for fifty to seventy dollars each. It cost the district a hundred each to replace them.

"Then the thieves, I'm betting the same ones," Dale continued angrily, "stole a bunch of sports equipment from our softball and baseball storage units. That happened over the long Labor Day weekend."

"Since then they've gotten bolder and entered the building," Lanell interjected. "Some laptops were stolen from the library. I understand that a nearby pharmacy was robbed last week," she added. "But that doesn't seem linked. Now their looting has escalated and a murder resulted. I don't think it's kids."

The detective nodded. "Those impressions coincide with mine. Thank you both for your time."

After the little group parted ways, Lanell went about her final round of the day, mentally going back over the entire day and her conclusions. As she crawled behind the wheel of her police cruiser to go home, two facts stood out in her mind.

This thievery, and the possibility of more violence, had to be stopped.

And the good looking man who had shown up to check on his former teacher was Carly Prescott's brother.

Chapter 2

During the meal that evening at the WhitakersConnor couldn't stop sneaking peeks at Lanell. Since her unexpected appearance, he hadn't quite caught his breath.

He didn't know what to think about his former mentor and her husband—his boss—inviting him and Carly, and the school resource officer, all to dinner—that just happened to be grilled chicken with the special marinade Dale knew he loved. He hadn't been able to catch her eye and read guilt or innocence. Surely she wasn't trying to play matchmaker. He had never known her to do such a thing.

It was a chatter punctuated meal, but not absorbing enough to keep Connor from being aware of Lanell's every move and word. He found himself wondering if she had anyone who claimed her affections, or if anyone ever shortened her name to just Nell. Dressed in black denim jeans and a fleecy blue top rather than being in uniform, she looked quite different, more approachable. Her dark blue eyes were framed by long dark lashes and gleamed with intelligence. Her face was a delicate oval, her skin fair and nearly flawless. She wore her honey-blond hair loose to her shoulders, making him wonder if it could possibly be as soft as it looked.

Suddenly he realized that the conversation had returned to the murder. He focused on what Dale was saying.

"After finding Vernon, Lanell told me to run back to the office and notify our principal. Then I had to meet students instead of going back to …" Her voice broke, and she looked upward, blinking back tears.

Connor understood her pain. After Vernon stayed with the Whitakers during the second half of his senior year and graduated from high school, he had kept in touch during college, and then returned to his home school as a teacher after getting his degree. This was his second year on the faculty.

"I couldn't tell the students anything, and seeing the ambulance and police cars had them asking questions constantly," she continued when she had regained her composure. "Even if I hadn't been told to withhold what I knew, I couldn't have talked about it."

From across the table Connor's sister aimed a look of understanding at her former coach. "We'll get whoever did it," Carly promised solemnly.

"Do you have any idea who it could have been?" Lanell asked, not looking directly at Carly.

Connor sensed unease between his sister and the resource officer. He didn't understand it. They both worked for the local police department. There didn't seem to be hostility between them, but there was definitely a lack of camaraderie. He couldn't help but wonder why—other than the fact that Carly was a rooky and Lanell a veteran. Was she a work snob?

"It's so hard to believe he's dead," Dale murmured,

shaking her head sadly.

Connor's heart twisted. Dale was taking this hard. "I'm trying to remember him as the great guy he was," he made himself say.

Justin reached over and placed a hand over his wife's. "I'm doing the same."

Connor watched the couple exchange forced smiles, and experienced a touch of envy. They had a loving relationship and a happy home, things he had forfeited years ago. His own experiences had not been of that caliber, and he didn't dare risk repeating the mistakes his parents had made.

"Have you learned any more about the burglary ring?" he asked Lanell, forcing her to face him. He sipped from his iced tea.

"It looks like all the shop tools of substantial value were stolen," she said tersely.

"Were there any surveillance cameras?"

"No," she said slowly, her eyes wary and watchful.

"How did the thieves get inside?"

She drew a long breath. "I can't discuss details of the investigation with non-law enforcement persons."

A little irritated, he succumbed to an imp of mischief. "So you're not going to tell me if you found any fingerprints or footprints of significance?"

She gave him a mouth tightening look. "No, I'm not. And you'd better not interfere in a police case."

A thump drew their attention. Carly had plunked her coffee mug on the table with force. "He's not interfering. He's just interested, like everyone in the school and neighborhood who have heard about the murder."

Connor raised his palms in the air. "I didn't mean

to cause a stir. Let's change the subject."

~

Guilt pricked at Lanell. She didn't understand why this guy nettled her so. And she shouldn't let her distrust of his sister ruin a simple dinner. Her mistake had been in letting Dale Whitaker convince her to come at all. The woman had been so insistent that she needed a support group around her that Lanell hadn't been able to refuse.

"Do any of you have any idea who could be behind the thievery that's plaguing the school?" she asked in a conciliatory tone.

Connor made no response. But Carly did.

"There has to be someone at the school involved. The crooks know where the most valuable and disposable goods are located."

"It could be former students," Justin said, contributing to the speculation. "Do you remember any who got in trouble for that kind of thing?" He directed the question at his wife.

Dale dabbed at her eyes and firmed her shoulders. "I don't recall anyone like that, but the school wouldn't have dealt with issues that occurred outside of school hours and off school property. The police would have handled it. I can't imagine anyone on our staff who would be involved in criminal activities, especially against the school."

Lanell watched the sad look that filled Dale's eyes. She was truly devastated. Hopefully she would be able to control her emotions enough to do her job when she returned to school tomorrow and had to hear coworkers and students discussing Vernon and speculating about who could have killed him.

Over the next ten minutes they tried to think of anything that would provide any answers. By that time, Lanell figured it was time to leave and rose from the table. “Thank you for the meal and the fellowship. I’ve enjoyed it, but I need to be going.”

Dale rose from her chair and rounded the table. “We’ve loved having you here, and I hope it won’t be your last visit with us.” She wrapped her arms around Lanell and hugged her. When she pulled away, her smile was back in place.

They walked to the front door, and Lanell claimed her coat from the rack in the foyer. “I’ll see you tomorrow,” she said quietly. “Chin up. We’re going to catch whoever did this.”

During the drive to her apartment, the snow flurries that had been intermittent all day built to a steady downfall of fluffy flakes. The sun had dipped below the horizon, the gray of dusk settling over the land like a shroud. The oldies music flowing from her car radio did little to distract her thoughts. She couldn’t stop thinking about the case—or Connor Prescott.

His dark eyes seemed to see right through her, but were hard—make that impossible—to read. She got the feeling that he looked more deeply at her than other men ever had, as if he knew her tough, cop-like exterior was a cover for feelings she preferred to keep private.

Shaking off the thoughts of him, she found them replaced by ones of his sister. Carly Prescott had only joined the force a few months ago, and Lanell knew almost nothing about her personal life. She seemed bright and capable, but Lanell had concerns about her. More than once she had observed Carly in the company of a woman of questionable character. Donna Echols and her husband spent a good deal of time in the local bars, and Donna's dad was suspected of shady dealings in the multiple businesses he owned.

Once again shaking off her preoccupation with the Prescott siblings, she pulled into the parking lot of the police station. She wanted to chat with Detective White, and found him working late, as promised when she called before driving away from the Whitaker home.

As she entered his office, he pushed a folder across the desk at her. It was a preliminary report from the medical examiner.

She sat, opened it, and began reading. It said Vernon had sustained blows about the head, the fatal one being the one to his temple. The doctor estimated death to have occurred between nine and midnight Sunday evening.

Over the next hour they went back over everything Lanell had done and seen that morning. When they finished, she was frustrated at being no closer to any answers than when she arrived.

"Let's sleep on it, and maybe we'll think better in the morning." Fatigue lacing his words, Evan closed the folder before him.

Lanell stood. "I'll keep my eyes and ears open at the campus."

Once at home in her apartment, she took a shower, dressed for bed, and turned on the television. A commercial for a pain reliever made her wish for a pill that would ease the pain of heartache. She changed the channel to a local one, anxious to hear how the news of the murder was being reported.

"This morning the resource officer and a teacher at Central High School found the body of an industrial arts teacher in his classroom. It is thought that Vernon Ziegler walked in on a robbery and was killed by the thieves."

The camera cut to Principal Blake Autry, who answered a few questions and assured the listening public that the authorities were doing everything in their power to apprehend the culprits.

Lanell turned off the set when the story ended. A sense of quiet settled over her as she gazed at the blank screen, thinking about Vernon Ziegler. Yesterday he had been a living, breathing twenty-five-year-old teacher. Today he was dead. Who had made him a murder statistic?

She thought about the people who worked at the school, visualizing them one by one, trying to picture who could be involved. And drew a blank.

She needed sleep—and time to think.

~

"When do you have to leave?" Carly asked as Connor pulled into the parking lot of the apartment complex where they lived with their dad.

"Six in the morning, and I'll be gone overnight." He had an overseas flight.

Carly had been living across town in an apartment of her own until she decided to abandon hairdressing and enter the police academy. Moving in with him had been a way of cutting her expenses until she could graduate and get acclimated to her new job.

She had been about ready to move out when their dad was released from prison and had no place to stay. The little house their family had lived in before Steve went to prison, and then Connor and Carly had lived in after their mother died, had been damaged beyond repair by a big storm a couple of years ago. They had seen no choice but to have it torn down.

They had talked over the situation and decided to invite Steve to live with them until he could get on his feet, and Carly would stay on if he accepted. The three of them had now been living here together for the past four months.

"Just a minute," he said when his sister started to get out of the vehicle. He didn't really want to bring up this subject, but he was concerned about her, and he didn't want to discuss it in Dad's hearing.

She paused, her hand on the door handle, and faced him. "What?"

He hauled in a deep breath. "Are you sure you know who you're hanging out with?"

Carly tipped her head back, telling him she was rolling her eyes, even though he couldn't see them clearly in the shadows.

"I'm a big girl now, Connor. So butt out."

His hands tightened on the wheel. "I wish I could. I know you're hurting right now, and I care about you. I need to know you're not getting involved with someone who'll draw you into something …"

"Illegal?" she cut him off angrily. Then the fight visibly drained from her. "You must have seen me with Donna Echols."

He drew a heavy breath. "After I left the gym Thursday night I saw you walking up the street with her, and you weren't in uniform. It's not the only time I've seen the two of you together. Donna always had bad taste in boyfriends when we were in high school together, and then in men later. She and her husband live in the bars, and I'm afraid they make their living dishonestly."

"That's right," Carly admitted. "It's her dad I'm after, though. Not in that way," she added quickly when he made a startled sound.

Connor considered her words. "Are you working on a case?"

She shrugged. "Yes and no. I'm convinced her dad's a crook, and I'm hoping to learn more about his businesses and the people who work for and with him."

"So you're cultivating a relationship to get information. Does your superior know what you're doing?"

"No." She hesitated before saying any more. "I think Donna's dad is reporting robberies that are faked, so he can collect insurance payouts."

"You think Donna's in on it?"

"I wasn't sure at first. I don't think so now. Her husband might be, though. I'm not sure."

"If you're not working for your department, why are you sticking your nose into the matter?"

Her hands clenched. "A friend of mine worked as a bookkeeper for Donna's dad, and she became worried when he had robberies in more than one business. Then she began noticing other things that didn't seem right. When she talked to her boss, he seemed to take her concerns to heart. But the next week Heidi was accused of forging a check on the company, and he fired her. She insists she didn't do it and asked my help to clear her name."

"So you're working your own case, on your own time," he said slowly. "Don't you realize that's dangerous?"

"I want to help Heidi," she said, gritting her teeth.

"And I also want to help Donna. I think she's being abused by her husband."

"Can't you talk to your captain about it?"

"I have no proof. And Donna won't report anything."

"Have you talked to any more experienced officers? What about Lanell?" He should have stopped before that last sentence.

"Maybe I should, but I don't know many of them well enough to seek them out. And I get the feeling that Lanell doesn't like me."

"Don't be too hard on her," he cautioned. "She doesn't know you well enough to not like you."

Carly went quiet, her attention focusing rigidly on him. After several long moments she erupted into speech. "Good grief. The sky's falling in. You're interested in her."

He turned in the seat and glared at her. "I tell you what. I'll drop the first subject, and you can drop that one."

A hand shot toward him. "Deal."

They shook hands and exited the vehicle.

Chapter 3

Tuesday morning Lanell arrived at the school early enough to visit the teachers' lounge for a donut and coffee before the day became busy. As she walked down the hall finishing the last bite of donut, she ignored the Christmas decorations beginning to appear in the offices, classrooms, and hallway nooks. They brought her no joy. She always dreaded the holiday season, and hated Christmas Day, the anniversary of her mother's death from a drug overdose.

She turned a corner and met two janitors. Eddie was pushing a mop bucket, while Claude toted a load of cleaning supplies. Both wore grumpy expressions.

"I don't see why we couldn't get this done yesterday," Eddie grumbled.

"What's up, guys?" Lanell asked in a friendly fashion.

Claude rolled his eyes. "We're on our way to clean the shop. It would have been easier yesterday when the mess was fresh. All that blood's bound to be dried and stuck to the floor by now."

These two were veteran complainers. If that hadn't been an excuse, there would have been another. They never lacked for them. She tried to block out the images they had revived.

"The police had to examine and document every aspect of the scene," she said diplomatically. "It's tedious work, and they had to take their time and be sure to cover everything."

Eddie edged over closer to her. "What was it like finding somebody dead that way?" he asked in a stage whisper.

"It was not a good experience," she said briefly, not about to get pulled into a gruesome gossip session with these guys. She glanced at her watch. "I have to get outside."

Armed with their buckets and scrub brushes, the janitors continued their way down the hall.

After monitoring arrival of the buses and students, Lanell decided to swing by the gym before classes started and see how Dale was getting along.

The teacher was sitting on the bottom bleacher, her grade book in her lap, staring morosely at the far wall. Lanell slid onto the bench beside her. "How are you doing?"

Having been lost in reverie, Dale's head whipped around, revealing a haunted expression. "Remembering. Grieving," she said hollowly. "Vernon's mother called early this morning. Her ex-husband is meeting her here this afternoon to deal with funeral arrangements. She wanted to know if I'll go to the funeral home with them after school."

Lanell placed an arm across Dale's shoulders. "You'll be a source of strength for them."

"No parent should have to endure this kind of loss," she said harshly, her hands clenched.

"No, they shouldn't. No one should."

They sat in silence for several moments. "You said Vernon was a senior when you took him into your home, so he didn't stay there long, did he?"

"No, but he was still special."

"And he wasn't the first. How old were Connor and Carly when they stayed with you?" She hoped a change of subject would help Dale get her bearings. And she was curious.

Her expression took on a look of long ago remembrance. "Connor was not quite eighteen, a senior, and Carly was a freshman. But they became independent and moved into their own place within weeks."

"But you still kept your eye on them, didn't you?"

Dale nodded, her face clearing a bit. "Connor was a very responsible young man. After their mother suffered a stroke and had to be placed in a nursing home, he and Carly had no choice but to move in with an aunt. Their dad was in prison. When their mother died a year or so later, the aunt decided to move to another town and informed them that they had to go with her. They didn't want to move, or change schools, and planned to run away."

Sympathy for the two young people they had been gripped Lanell's heart.

"The only transportation they had was a bicycle, and it got damaged in an accident. But Justin's brother who has a car dealership in Branson awarded Connor a car for his outstanding scholarship and character, and the husband of a friend of mine gave Carly a job. Both teens worked hard and stayed with me until their mother's little house was repaired enough for them to live in it. Their dad signed the paperwork needed for Connor to become emancipated and be made Carly's guardian. After his high school graduation, he attended college here in Springfield while she finished high school. Then he did a stint in the Air Force. I'm proud of both of them."

Lanell swallowed hard. They had endured a lot, but overcome great odds against them. She thought she understood both of them better now.

"What kind of work does Connor do?"

Dale grinned. "He's a pilot, and the safety officer, for Justin's charter airline. Carly became a hairdresser, but didn't find it as satisfying as she had expected and applied to the police academy after only a few months. After getting accepted, she stayed with Connor while going through training. Recently their dad was released from prison and moved in with them."

Lanell's mind went into a spin. They had a felon living with them? Could he be involved in the robberies? "When was he released?"

"Four months ago."

"When did the school thefts begin?" she murmured to herself, thinking back and correlating the time frame. It fit.

Dale's expression turned to one of dismay. "Mr. Prescott's not involved in anything illegal. He wouldn't be. I'm sure of it."

Lanell wasn't sure how to respond. But she didn't have to. The ringing of the bell for the beginning of classes was welcome.

~

"What do you know about the killing at that school?" his dad asked as Connor entered the apartment.

Connor closed the door and began to remove his gloves and coat. Steve sat on the sofa facing the muted TV he had obviously been watching, gripping the remote in his right hand. Slightly above medium height, his skin was pale, his hair graying and thinning. He wore a new red shirt and jeans that had been his first purchase after being released from prison and returning to Springfield.

"The victim was a young teacher who received help from a veteran teacher when he was in high school. She and the resource officer are the ones who found him."

Sighing deeply, Connor hung his coat on the coat tree and crossed the room to a chair facing his dad. The scent of something cooking drifted from the kitchen, making his stomach growl.

"Was it the same teacher who befriended you and Carly?"

He nodded, wondering how Steve had sensed that.

"How is she handling it?"

"It has hit her hard. I don't remember Vernon very well, but Carly does. They were in the same grade, and they had been dating recently. If Dale found him worthy of taking under her wing, he had to be okay."

"I assume the resource officer is dealing with it better than the teacher."

A vision of her slender, blond beauty made him grin slightly. "She's a take-charge, stay-out-of-my-way lady. I'm counting on her to nail the killer."

His dad shifted and leaned forward a bit. "It sounds like you're impressed with her."

Connor shrugged, attempting nonchalance. "I

guess."

Steve's mouth curved a tiny bit. "Okay, I get it. You don't want to talk about her."

Connor inhaled the aroma drifting from the kitchen. "What are you doing home so early?"

Their shifts seldom coincided. His dad worked seven to four and returned to the apartment around five. Connor's schedule was supposed to be eight to five, but often varied. Today he had made a short flight to Nevada, grabbed a quick lunch and nap, flown his clients home from their morning business meetings by three o'clock, and then worked in the office until five.

Steve frowned. "Work is slow. We were between jobs today, but they had me work in the shop this morning. I got home about two, so I started a pot of stew for supper."

He was working for a roofing company, and it was hot, dirty work. Tar was boiled in a cooker and often spattered on them, burning deeply into their skin. They climbed up and down to and from rooftops and endured blistering heat in the summer, frigid cold in the winter, and lost work when it rained.

"The boss told us today that he just contracted a big school job, but it won't start until the end of the school term."

Connor studied his dad's stress lined, perpetually solemn face. He couldn't remember ever seeing him smile. Carly was currently on second shift, so was at work and wouldn't be home until midnight.

"I've got a heavy schedule next week, and Carly's grabbing all the overtime she can because she wants the money. I don't see how either of us is going to have time to put up the Christmas tree. How about we surprise her and put it up after supper?"

"If you want," Steve said without enthusiasm and pushed to his feet.

After generous helpings of stew and cornbread, Connor went to the hall closet and dug out the extra tall artificial tree he had found on sale after Christmas last year. It already had lights on it, so all they had to do was assemble it. Once they had it together, he used the kitchen step stool to place the star at the top. As he turned to step off the stool, it tipped, throwing him off balance. A hand instinctively shot out and grabbed for support, latching onto a tree branch. The entire tree toppled backward with him, and he tumbled into his dad. They landed in a pile, tree branches covering them.

Connor turned his head, and locked gazes with Steve. There was a long moment of silence. Then his dad drawled, "You're supposed to deck the halls, not deck your dad."

Taken by surprise at the bit of wry humor, Connor wasn't sure how to respond. But it was unnecessary as he heard a sound that was music to his ears.

His dad laughed.

~

Wednesday morning's assembly in the gym was a solemn affair. The superintendent opened it and beseeched anyone who knew anything that could help the police identify Vernon's killer to share the information with them. Then he turned the meeting over to the principal.

After offering the students some suggestions for dealing with their grief—seeking a place to go to be alone and quiet, things to read, and seeing the counselor—Blake Autry allowed a short time of silence to remember Vernon. Then the music teacher sang a couple of Vernon's favorite songs, and everyone filed silently out of the room.

After lunch, Lanell patrolled the building and grounds and returned to her little office. She had just booted her computer when a tap at the door made her look up. When Becky Phillips opened the door a crack and peered through the tiny opening, Lanell beckoned for the student to enter.

The girl entered timidly. She wore shorts and a tee shirt, indicating she had come from P.E. class. She carried a miniature softball bat that Lanell knew was etched with Dale Whitaker's name and served as her hall pass.

"What can I do for you, Becky?" She pointed at the chair at the end of her desk.

Becky sidled onto it and clasped her hands together around the little wooden bat. "I'm not sure I should be here," she began hesitantly. "I didn't want the other kids to know where I was going, so I asked Coach Whitaker during lunch if I could use her bathroom pass to come see you during class."

Lanell leaned forward. "Do you know something about what happened to Mr. Ziegler?"

Becky frowned and drew a deep breath. "I don't know, but Coach said I should talk to you."

"Don't be nervous. Just tell me what's bothering you. I promise the other students won't know you spoke with me."

That seemed to relax her a bit. "My brother says the guys were talking in the locker room before Monday night's basketball game, and somebody said Grant Overton isn't coming back to school."

Three weeks ago Grant had been suspended for the rest of the semester. He had been stealing money from clothing carelessly left in the locker room, and breaking into lockers. He was eventually caught.

"What's the significance?"

Becky raked her teeth over her bottom lip. "Brad said Grant told some guys he's making too much money to bother with school anymore."

Brad was Becky's brother. "Do you and Brad think he's making so much money because he's hooked up with the burglary ring that's hitting the schools?"

Shrugging, Becky looked down and smoothed a hand over the little wooden bat. "We have no way of knowing for sure, but it sounds like the kind of thing Grant would do."

Lanell nodded in understanding. "It bears checking out. Thank you for sharing your concerns with me."

After Becky left, Lanell eased back in her chair and pondered the validity of this information. Then she turned to her computer and sent an email to Detective White, relaying what Becky had told her.

Police officers attend funerals of murder victims to see who does and does not attend. According to statistics, most murder victims are killed by someone they know, and that person will often attend the funeral, fearing that his/her absence will throw suspicion on him or her. On the other hand, sometimes the killer is a stranger who attends because he or she derives a sense of power by being there without anyone guessing his or her identity.

Even if Lanell had not known this—and been assigned the Thursday duty—she would have been at this one. She sat in a pew near the rear where she could be inconspicuous and have a good view of the entire area.

Thankfully, the day was a couple of degrees warmer than it had been all week, and the sun had appeared. Hopefully it would stay visible until after the services.

As a soloist sang a hymn, Lanell watched Dale, who was seated next to her husband directly behind Vernon's parents, who sat on the same front pew, but with space between them. A range of emotions played across Dale's face—grief, bewilderment, anger. She stared forward, lost in her mental world. When she returned to the present, she turned her head enough to glance back at Lanell. The message she sent was, *Get whoever did this.*

Lanell nodded slightly, indicating it would be done.

As the pastor painted a picture of heaven and assured the mourners that Vernon was there, people sat stone silent, tears leaking from eyes and trickling down cheeks.

At the end of the service, he quoted the twenty-third Psalm. After people filed past the casket, they got in their vehicles and drove in a procession behind the hearse to the cemetery, where a final eulogy, prayer, and good-byes were said.

Lanell returned to her apartment none the wiser. She had observed those present, but noticed no one who seemed out of place or acting odd. A high percentage of school personnel had been present, along with Vernon's extended family and friends.

She tried to review the events of the day in her mind, but Connor's face imposed itself over everything. Forcing her thoughts back to business, she mentally reviewed the murder scene.

Vernon had died in his own space, in a senseless act of violence. He had been lying on the floor not far from the entrance, a hammer near him.

Work tables had been bare of valuable equipment. The thieves had apparently been about ready to leave, and Vernon's unexpected arrival had thrown them into a panic. One of them had grabbed a hammer and attacked Vernon from behind.

The medical examiner's report indicated the cruel act had been committed sometime between nine and twelve Sunday night. Who could have entered through the door with a key and broken the window in an attempt to make it look like they had gotten inside through it so no one would realize they had a key? Where could they have gotten a key?

Who all had keys? Staff members had keys to their own classrooms and labs. Administrators had keys to everything. Maintenance and cleaning crews had keys to all the places they worked.

The list seemed endless. It was the detective's job to follow up on clues and interview suspects. She had daily access to these people, so she had to do some investigating, consider everyone a suspect, and share her information with the detective.

Friday morning after students arrived and classes began, Lanell patrolled the halls, working her way toward her little office to make some phone calls. For starters she wanted to talk to Detective White again and find out if he had formed any more conclusions.

She turned a corner and met Claude. He stopped his rolling mop bucket when he came alongside her. His shirt hung limply on bony shoulders, and brown pants rested low on his narrow hips. He formed an exaggerated grimace. "Will you accompany me to the girls' locker room while they're out in the gym having class? Mrs. Whitaker called and asked me to mop up where one of the girls got sick and lost her stomach. Eddie said he'll get sick if he has to mop puke. He's a wimp."

Lanell laughed. "Lead the way."

Inside the locker room, she leaned against the door while Claude cleaned up the mess. "I've noticed how well you look after Mrs. Whitaker and the gym," she said to his hunched over form.

The man rose up and turned to lean on the mop handle. "She's a nice lady. I don't mind doing little extras for her. You should have seen us paint signs for the cancer pink out day back in October. We both ended up with paint all over us."

Lanell looked him over thoroughly, thinking of his familiarity with the building. "Do you have any idea who is robbing from the school and killed Vernon?"

A wary look flashed over his face at the sudden question. But he recovered quickly. "I've thought about it, but I can't think of anyone around here who would be involved in something like that. Do you want me to start asking around and see what I can find out?"

His eagerness was surprising. "It wouldn't hurt to keep your eyes and ears open, but don't question anyone."

He returned to his task and finished quickly. As he left the room, Lanell turned in the opposite direction and headed toward her office.

Lord, if You care about these people, help us bring the killer to justice.

Chapter 4

Connor was tired when he arrived home after a long day fraught with scheduling snags, a missed lunch, and disgruntled people.

"Carly had to go in early to relieve someone who got sick at work," Steve said as Connor removed his coat in the foyer. "Do you have to go back out tonight?"

"I don't have to, but I need to," he answered as he entered the living room. "Basketball season opens this week at the school, and tonight there's an exhibition game between the team players and faculty members. Would you like to go with me?"

Steve frowned across the room at him. "I'd like to, but I'm too tired. We actually worked a full shift today. I have a pot of chili about ready if you're interested."

Connor grinned and rolled his eyes. "You bother to ask?"

His dad returned the grin, which made Connor feel better about leaving him behind. He had worried that Steve was dodging human contact as much as possible, but his new level of relaxation indicated he was turning down tonight's outing because he was truly tired, not that he couldn't face the public.

"I'll set the table and make tea," he said.

"Will your favorite teacher be playing?" Steve asked when they were about done eating.

Connor nodded. "Yep. That means she could probably use help corralling her little ones."

"Her husband is your boss. Do I have that right?"

Connor nodded again.

"Well, won't he be there to look after them?"

"Yes, but he'll be late. He's clearing up some matters at the airport. I told him I'll lasso Jennifer and Jaxson until he gets there."

"How old are they?"

Connor smiled, visualizing their pixie faces. "Jennifer is three. Jax is one."

"Sounds like fun." His dad's wry expression said otherwise.

Connor cleared his throat. "Dad, there's something I've been meaning to ask you."

Steve leaned back in the chair. "Well, ask."

"I've had an inquiry from someone interested in buying the lot you own. Do you want to sell it, or do you think you might like to build on it someday, or maybe buy a trailer and put on it?"

Steve gave him a long, searching look. "Don't fret over anything you had to do, Son. Why don't you sell the property and consider whatever you get for it as payment for all you've done over the years? It's not much, but maybe it …"

Connor lifted a palm for silence. "No, it's your property. I'm fine, and so is Carly. Don't worry about us."

"But you should have it."

"Fine," Connor said in exasperation. "We'll sell it, but I don't want the money."

"And I do, huh?" Steve's mouth quirked a bit. "Are we gonna fight about it?"

Connor wiped his mouth on a napkin and tossed it down. "I don't have time to fight with you. I'll tell the buyer to talk to you."

He exchanged his uniform for jeans and a heavy sweatshirt, grabbed his coat, and headed out into the night. A few flakes of snow were still floating down, but there was no sign of the predicted severe weather.

By the time he walked into the gym, Connor had pushed the matter of the property to the back of his mind. He would do nothing, forcing his dad to make a decision about whether to sell it or do something else with it. He thought he had detected a spark of interest when he mentioned the idea of buying a trailer. Steve needed time. Ten years in prison had taken its toll on him.

Dale Whitaker met him inside the school's front entrance. "I've already paid for you," she said, tilting her head toward the ticket takers at the table to the left of the principal's office door.

Connor shook his head. She knew how he felt about taking money from her—for anything. "I'm well paid," he said, reaching for the infant carrier she lifted toward him.

Jennifer clutched his knee, gazing up at him. "Connor, are you taking care of me and Jax? Please say yes."

He wrinkled his nose at her. "Yes. Your daddy will be here before long."

"Well, I have to go." Dale handed him a diaper bag, turned, and marched up the hallway.

Between Jennifer's chatter and the mob in the hall,

they made it to the gym and found a seat on the second row of bleachers, near the floor where he wouldn't have to run up and down them with these two. Fortunately, the spot on the bottom row directly in front of them was vacant.

It was near the end of the first half of the first game, the girls' team against the women faculty, when Justin Whitaker slid onto the bench next to Connor.

"Daddy, take Jaxie," Jennifer ordered.

Justin took the baby from Connor, and Jennifer immediately climbed onto Connor's vacated lap. He didn't know how to react when she snuggled up against him.

"You need some of these," Justin whispered in his ear.

"It takes two," Connor pointed out somewhat brusquely.

"So get married," Justin said, unperturbed. "Hey, did you see that?"

Connor looked up at the scoreboard just in time to see the score increase by three points. A quick glance back at the floor confirmed that Dale had made the basket.

They focused on the game, interspersed with Jennifer's demands for explanations and Jax's for attention.

"Dale said a janitor by the name of Claude told her he wants to surprise his woman for Christmas and needs to see Dale outside of school hours about it," Justin said during a lull. "He didn't explain, just said he wants to bring his woman to meet her tonight. But he said he couldn't get here until the second game."

~

After the first game ended, Lanell spotted Dale and her family, and decided to get off her feet for a bit. She rounded the gym floor and slid onto the bench beside the teacher she was growing fonder of every day.

To her surprise, three-year-old Jennifer left Mr. Prescott's lap, bypassed her dad, and scooted onto Lanell's lap. She had no experience with children and was unsure how to respond. But when Jennifer's warm little body snuggled close, the pixie haired tyke stole her heart in a breathtaking rush of emotion.

Lanell smiled down at the child's delicate face. She was beautiful. Her tiny bow mouth curved into a smile. "I like you," she said with a slight lisp. "Mommy says you keep us safe."

"I'm part of the police force that works to do that," Lanell explained, finding herself thinking it would be nice to have such a child of her own.

Maybe someday she would. She had never dwelt on the idea, always thinking there would be time later to consider it when she had her career on track—and decide whether she wanted a family enough to risk a serious relationship.

But time had slipped away. She was focused on her job, locked into a pattern of life, and seldom dated. Make that never dated. She studiously ignored Connor Prescott, not too hard to do with Dale and Justin sitting between them.

As the boys' team and men faculty began to play, she spied Claude and a female companion pausing inside the doorway and then coming toward them. The sound of a gasp made her turn to face Dale.

The teacher's face had blanched. And her wide-eyed expression indicated utter shock.

Lanell followed Dale's line of vision. It seemed to be focused on the woman with Claude. "Do you know her?" she asked quietly.

"It's my … my mother," she said haltingly, sitting rigid and still as stone and staring at the heavyset woman with graying hair as if she couldn't believe her eyes.

Her mother? So why did she look like she was seeing a ghost?

Lanell knew almost nothing about Dale's background or family life, other than she had a twin brother who worked at her husband's charter airline. Such a reaction at sight of her mother was beyond understanding.

When the couple halted before them, the sallow complexioned woman leaned on her cane and tipped her head to study Dale. Creases lined her deep-set eyes. "I might not have recognized you, but you look as good as Claude said."

Lanell couldn't keep from asking, "Has it been a long time since you've seen her?"

"Not since I was a teenager," Dale said in a low, strained voice.

Lanell swallowed a gasp. She had to mean twenty years or more.

"That's right," the woman said, as if that were normal. "I've changed quite a bit since then. Do you mind if we sit here?" She nodded at the empty spot on the front bench before them.

"Of course not," Dale said, her voice stronger now that she had had a few moments to absorb her obvious shock.

Claude helped his companion ease her full figure

onto the bench before them. At that moment a loose ball came flying toward them, a player chasing it. The boy bumped Claude's shoulder. "Sorry," he yelled, grabbing the ball.

"No problem," Claude returned, seeming unfazed and plunking down beside …whatever the woman's name was.

Moments later she heard Claude address her as Leona. Lanell stood and placed Jennifer next to her daddy. "You all are great company, but I'm on duty, and I've been stationary long enough. See you around."

She stepped between Claude and the man to his left, hopped to the floor, and continued her surveillance rounds. But she glanced over at Dale's little group each time she was inside the gym rather than patrolling the halls. She didn't notice much interaction, and wondered what kind of relationship existed there.

~

Claude's surprise was bringing his woman to meet her daughter?

Connor debated whether he should find another seat, but when he made a move to stand, Justin placed a hand on his arm and gave a head shake to signal him to stay. He hated being an intruder in their family reunion, but Justin was his boss, and he seemed to want him there. Connor reached for the baby. At least he could do that much, and let Justin focus on his wife.

"I want to sit with Connor," Jennifer informed her dad, wiggling back past her dad.

"I can handle both," Connor said quickly, knowing Justin would not hand him a second kid unless persuaded.

His boss rolled his eyes, as if saying Connor didn't

know what he was doing. But he allowed Jennifer to crawl onto Connor's free knee.

Jennifer reached up and clasped her little hands around his face. "I like you, Connor. Will you take me to walk?"

The game had started, so he hesitated. But when she squirmed in a certain way, he grimaced at his boss. "If you'll take this smaller critter back, I'll take her out into the hall and find a girl who'll take her to the restroom."

Justin took the carrier. "It's a deal," he said before his wife could object.

Connor took Jennifer in his arms and left the gym. He quickly found a familiar teen willing to take the tot where she needed to go. When they returned, he took Jennifer by the hand and walked her up and down the hallway until she had burned off some of her restless energy. Then they returned to the gym.

"You need one of your own," Justin repeated softly as they resumed their seat.

The idea held an unprecedented appeal, but Connor wasn't willing to open a discussion about his love life—or lack thereof. So he ignored the comment.

Dale's mother turned around to face her. "You should bring your family to visit me and Claude, give us a chance to get to know those little ones."

"Sometime," Dale responded vaguely. "How are you doing?"

The woman frowned. "Well, my diabetes is pretty serious, and my knees don't hold me up very well, but I'm getting along."

Something about her tone and manner made Connor suspect that she was seeking sympathy.

"We can't afford insurance," the woman continued, and started to say more, but was interrupted by a rush of action on the floor near them.

Connor divided his attention between the game and Jennifer. He had gotten her a lollipop from the concession stand, and she scooted onto the wooden surface by his feet to eat it. When the game ended, he stayed seated while Claude and Dale's mother said their good-byes—with no hugs or intimate touches, he couldn't help but note—and left. Then he picked up the child, accompanied her parents to their vehicle, and put Jennifer in her car seat.

As they drove away, he started to his own vehicle, but changed his mind and returned to the school building. At the gym door he peeked inside and spotted Lanell Rhodes at one side of the huge room, talking to the principal. Connor returned to a spot near the exit and waited.

When Lanell appeared and took up a post near the doorway, he stepped over next to her—and caught the clean smell of her scented shampoo.

He licked his suddenly dry lips. She was near enough to touch, and he experienced an urge to do just that. It shook him with its intensity.

She gazed into his eyes, and the pupils darkened, telling him that this strange and unexpected reaction between them was not one sided.

He closed his eyes and breathed deeply, breaking the connection. This was insane.

She crossed her arms over her chest and leaned back. "Is there something on your mind?"

He nodded, gathering his wits. "You hungry?"

Her face creased. "That's what's on your mind?"

"Some tacos sound good, and the atmosphere would be more private."

Her gaze locked on him. "Tacos and talk?"

He felt off balance. "Yeah. Can you?"

She considered for a moment. "I have to stay until this place is locked up for the night."

"No problem. I'll wait in my vehicle and have it warm."

Fifteen minutes later they parked in the lot of a popular taco joint and went inside. They ordered, waited for their number to be called, and took their food and drinks to a booth.

"Let's eat, and then talk," he said after bowing his head, saying silent thanks for the food, and asking God for help with the talk.

They settled in to eat, making occasional comments about the food.

"Okay, what's on your mind?" she asked, wiping her mouth with a napkin.

"I'm concerned about Dale," he said, pushing his debris onto the tray at the side of the table.

Her eyes narrowed. "Why?"

Now that he had her attention riveted on him, he questioned his impulse to discuss this with her. He opted for a question. "Do you know anything about Dale's background?"

"No, but I admit tonight made me curious. I take it you do. Are you going to tell me?"

"You genuinely like her, don't you?" he asked instead of answering.

"Of course I do. She's one of the best."

He relaxed a bit. "She is."

Lanell raised a palm. "For the sake of disclosure,

I'll admit that she told me a bit about you and your sister staying with her briefly after your mother died."

He wasn't sure how he felt about that. Sharing his background always made him uncomfortable. But it made him feel a little better about discussing Dale. "She had a difficult background. One time when Carly and I were feeling kind of sorry for ourselves, she told us about it."

Lanell leaned forward on her arms. "I'm listening."

"Her mother was twice divorced. After that she drifted from one relationship to another, invariably choosing men of a shiftless nature."

"What about their father?"

"The twins were the product of the first marriage. Their parents divorced when Dale and Derek were babies. He disappeared and never contributed to their support. Dale said they have no idea if he's even still alive. The mother was an alcoholic and left her children alone a lot. They had a kind neighbor lady who kept an eye on them and found ways to keep them off the streets. Her son coached the Little League teams on which his sons played, and he included Dale and Derek. Derek pitched, and Dale was his catcher," he added with a chuckle.

Lanell's face lost its lines of tension. "So she played with the boys and became an outstanding athlete."

He nodded in a jerky fashion. "Yes. The neighbor lady became a surrogate mother to them, and when their mother left for good, the neighbor took them in and made Derek her handyman and Dale her kitchen assistant so they wouldn't feel like charity cases. When she died, she left her little house to them. Her own sons approved, since they didn't need it and loved the twins. Their mother had sold her home just before she disappeared."

"And Dale hadn't seen her mother since then," Lanell said slowly, obviously picturing tonight's scene and speculating. "Why do you think she showed up now?"

"I have nothing to go on but my instincts," he said slowly, "but I suspect her return is because she found out that her kids have done well."

She leaned forward. "You're afraid she's after more than just assurance that they're okay."

She was intuitive. "Yes."

Her eyes locked on his. "You don't think she means to harm them, do you?"

He shrugged. "I'm more inclined to think she wants to wheedle money from them. She thinks they have it, and she wants it."

"How do you think she plans to get it?"

He drew a deep breath. "I don't know. She may have had her boyfriend apply for a job here at the school so he could meet Dale and reunite them. I sense she's exaggerating, or feigning, her health issues."

"So they'll feel sorry for her?" she added, nodding pensively.

He nodded. "Milking it so they'll give her money for medical bills that may or may not not exist."

"And there will be other bills they can't pay," she added, following his line of thought.

"I hate feeling this way," he said. "But as I watched them tonight, this uneasy feeling kept growing in me. Even the timing seems suspect."

She eyed him keenly. "You mean because it's near

Christmas, when people are focused on giving?"

He shrugged. "It occurred to me. I think Dale needs protection, and I don't know any way to provide it. There's nothing but my gut feelings, so I can't go to the police about it."

A grin slowly worked its way across her face. "But you just did." She aimed a pointed look at her badge.

He slapped a hand over his eyes for a moment. "I hadn't seen it like that."

"It's okay. I don't think your feelings are crazy, and I'm in a position to keep an eye on her during the week days, maybe ask a question or two here and there."

"Are you on duty at all these games?"

"Most of them. Attending school functions is part of my job."

"When's the next one?"

"Monday night. Would you like me to get you a game schedule?"

"That would be great. How about I attend Monday night? You can give it to me then, and we can talk more about this over a snack later."

She considered for a moment. "Okay."

Chapter 5

Lanell was off duty on weekends, a definite plus of her assignment, and a major reason she had signed the list of applicants when the position had come open. Police schedules rotated between days, evenings, and midnight shifts, including weekends. Her energy level had improved since going to a consistent routine a little over a year and a half ago. She worked here during the entire school term, but returned to regular patrol duty—or became an office flunky—during the summers.

So far this week had produced a lot of heartache and questions. Staff and administrators had been interviewed, but no answers or clear insights had been forthcoming regarding Vernon's killer. Lanell shook off the depressing thought and polished off the rest of her cinnamon roll.

Her eyes swept the room—that could use a different kind of sweeping—and dusting. She sipped her coffee, unable to focus on house cleaning or the grocery shopping she needed to do. Instead, her thoughts gravitated back to images of Connor Prescott. The attachment that had been developing for Dale Whitaker seemed to be expanding to her immediate family and unofficially adopted members—that included Connor.

With a sigh of resolution Lanell concluded that grocery shopping had to be her top priority for the morning, put her shopping list in her purse, and left the apartment. On the way to the supermarket, it was as if her car took on a mind of its own, turned right instead of left, and ended up at the police station.

She went to Detective White's office and tapped on the door.

"Come in," he called from behind it.

She opened the door and peeked inside. "I wasn't sure if you were working today."

He waved her inside. "Yeah, I've got the weekend. What's on your mind—as if I didn't know."

She took a seat facing him across the desk. "Are you going to tell me if you've made any progress on our school murder case?"

He grimaced and tapped a finger on the folder she assumed was the crime scene report. "I wish I had. I've been going over the lab reports and interview notes, but nothing's clicking. The lab techs got a partial print from the hammer handle, and it's a match to an unknown set found at another school robbery, but all I can deduce from that is it's the same gang."

"What about Grant Overton, the suspended student? Have you had any luck there?"

"We tracked him down, but we can't tie him to our school burglaries. He produced a phone video of himself at a party. The time shown on the phone falls within the range of the crime, and others at the party vouch that he was there all evening."

"So he's off the hook."

"We'll keep him under our radar, but it looks like he's clear on this incident." His tone implied he wasn't so clear on something else.

Lanell pulled a folded sheet of paper from her purse. "I made separate lists of all certified and non-certified staff at the school."

"I'm looking into their backgrounds as I have time."

"I take it you haven't found anything that sets off alarms."

He gave a slight shake of his head. "No, but I'm convinced that someone is working with a team of burglars. You're not the only school that's being hit, so I'm guessing there's a connection, an inside person at each place."

"If one school figures out who they have in their employ who's tied to a burglary ring, a connection could be made to whoever it is in the others. So we need to concentrate on persons hired this year."

"That's my feeling."

She slid her sheet of paper across the desk to him. "If you'll mark the ones you've already checked, I have some time I could spend on the computer."

"Police resources, but on your time, huh?" He grinned. But he took the paper and began marking on it. "I started with non-certified," he admitted ruefully, "but I should have looked at hire dates. I wasn't thinking right."

Lanell picked up the paper when he slid it back, and did a quick scan of the ones he had marked. "Before I leave, I'll let you know who I've checked and if I've found anything useful."

Two hours later she handed him her list of notes

and left. One of the newer cooks had an arrest record, but no other new hires from her school had anything suspicious in their backgrounds, including Eddie Salinger. The middle-aged janitor was such a grumpy, sly acting guy that she had half expected to find a record of some kind on him.

Out of curiosity she had done some digging on Dale Whitaker's mother and her janitor boyfriend. After looking up Dale's records and finding that her maiden name was Denning, she had searched for Leona Denning and found that the woman still used that name. Raised in Missouri, she had a list of former addresses in several states, but had returned to the area during the past summer and now had an address in Aurora.

All she found on the current boyfriend was a spotty work record, and the fact that he had also grown up in the local area.

Discouraged, she headed to the supermarket.

~

Sunday morning, Connor and Carly sat in their usual pew at church, near the back in case Carly should get an emergency call and have to leave the service. He had invited their dad—again—to come with them, but Steve had declined—again. The best his invitation had gotten was Steve's usual, "Maybe later."

Seeing that the service was about to begin, Connor opened his mouth to sing along with the opening song, but movement in the aisle made him glance over. To his surprise, Steve slid into the pew beside him. Carly reached across his lap to pat their dad's hand.

"Glad you made it," she whispered, smiling brightly.

Connor's heart gladdened. He wasn't sure where

their dad's relationship with the Lord stood, but he prayed that it would take root and grow.

When the service ended, some attendees left quickly, but others took time to chat in the aisle or in small clusters near the outer walls of the sanctuary. A local, mid-forties woman who taught art at the high school approached them. Her shoulder length hair was platinum blond, with a wide black swath of bangs that draped across her forehead and down over her right ear in her distinctive artistic flair. "It's good to see you two here at the same time, and that you have a guest with you," she said. Their schedules didn't always make that possible.

"Jazzy, I'd like you to meet our dad, Steve Prescott. Dad, this is Jasmine Dwyer."

Steve nodded and, somewhat awkwardly, extended a hand. "Pleased to meet you, Ma'am."

"I'm happy to meet you, Mr. Prescott. Welcome to our church. We hope you'll become a regular." She excused herself and left.

When Carly suggested they eat at the Golden Corral, Connor noted a spark in Steve's eyes—and the way his gaze followed Jazzy's exit. "Sounds good to me. Why don't we go in my vehicle? I'll bring you back here for yours," he said to his dad.

Steve shrugged and headed to the exit.

"I've decided to keep the property," he announced on the way to the restaurant. "I can't afford to build a house, but I might be able to buy a trailer in a few months, if I get regular work."

~

Lanell washed her hands and left the bathroom. Staff and students were beginning to fill the school building. Locker doors clanged, and Monday morning greetings and chatter echoed through the hallways.

She saw Eddie and Claude exit the gym, both pushing industrial dust mops. Lanell assumed they had just finished putting a shine to the floor. They were carrying on a conversation and didn't notice her behind them.

"He's not cut out for the job," Claude said.

"But he thinks he's hot stuff." Eddie's response sounded surly and condescending. "I wish I could have a private talk with him out behind the building. I'd show him a thing or two."

Lanell didn't know who they were discussing, but suspected it was the head of maintenance, a man who went to great lengths to treat employees fairly, including them. The tone of the discussion did nothing positive for her respect for the two men.

They stepped aside when the librarian came pushing a cart of books past them. When they did, they noticed Lanell.

"Morning," Claude greeted her. "How are you?"

"More wide awake now that I've had a cup of coffee."

Both men eyed her closely, probably wanting to ask questions about the murder investigation. She had no intention of sharing anything with them, even if she could.

"I'm hearing that parents are thinking of keeping their kids home from school," Eddie said. "Even with you here, they're worried that they ain't safe."

Claude nodded agreement. "I've heard the talk, too."

Lanell would not be drawn into the debate. "I have

to check on the breakfast crowd." She headed toward the cafeteria.

Dale Whitaker was on duty. She stood by the south wall, clutching a paper cup of coffee, and keeping watch over the students sitting at tables or moving about the room.

"I worry about so many of them," she said as Lanell approached, indicating the students with a head nod.

"You mean their safety?"

"Oh, that's important, but not what I meant. Many of them don't have adequate supplies or warm coats. My Sunday School class is conducting a coat drive, and they're going to send what they collect to the counselor here at the school."

"That sounds great."

Dale eyed her more carefully. "Do you happen to have an older coat that's in good shape and you don't wear anymore?"

Lanell's mind whirled. "I believe I do. I bet if I let the need be known at the police station, some of the officers would donate coats."

Dale's face brightened. "That would be great."

Lanell turned to walk away, but Dale touched her arm to stop her. She tipped her head and produced a mock look of pleading. "If you're free Friday night, would you consider helping us work on the athletic department's float for the Christmas parade then?"

The idea didn't hold a lot of appeal, but furthering her friendship with Dale did. "I might consider that," she said in a tone that said she was teasing and would be there.

"The art teacher has offered to help with the

banners to go on the sides of the float, and we'll be working in her garage. One of the coaches has rounded up a hay wagon for us to use. Will you be at the game tonight?"

"Yep." Lanell turned and moseyed on her way.

She made rounds and ended up in her little cubbyhole of an office, where she spent the next hour consuming a salad she had picked up from the cafeteria and doing computer research on personnel—with no significant results.

That evening she bagged a coat from her closet that she hadn't worn in ages and took it with her back to the school. Being the opening game of the season, she expected a high turnout—and was not disappointed. She automatically scanned the premises, looking for anything unusual or out of place, always on duty. She grabbed the bag from the passenger seat and headed inside.

As she walked up the sidewalk and into the building, Lanell wondered if Connor Prescott would be present. A knot formed in her stomach. Why did it matter? He was a pain in the neck.

Inside the gym, she did a quick survey, and located Dale and her family—including the prodigal mother. Claude was not with the woman, so Lanell guessed he was around somewhere, maybe working. He worked days, but sometimes filled in for a night shift janitor who was absent, or when they just needed extra help for bigger events.

She took the bagged coat to Dale, said a quick hello, and went to a position near the doorway where she kept watch for problems. Her gaze drifted periodically to the Whitaker bench, unable to shake the sense of unease generated by the sight of the mother. It wasn't so much her appearance, but something about her manner, that was disturbing. After more than twenty years of absence, the woman was fawning over Dale's babies and taking pains to put herself in their space. Connor was correct. It didn't feel right.

When the game started, Lanell left the gym and roamed the front halls where latecomers were still straggling inside. Bringing up the rear of those latecomers was Connor Prescott. She grinned and glanced at her watch as he approached the admission table.

"I've been all over the world today," he said when he had paid and walked over to where she stood. "Well, maybe only part of the world," he qualified with a rocking motion of his hand.

She shook her head at his silliness. "Your gang is sitting in almost the same spot they were in Friday night."

He started to move on, but paused. "Want to get a burger after the games?"

She did, but knew it probably wasn't a good idea. "Sure," she said, and nearly swallowed her tongue. She opened her mouth to retract the agreement, but stood staring at his back as he went on inside the gym, a bewildering flutter tickling her stomach. "We'll each drive our own vehicles," she called after him.

When they walked into a popular burger place after the games, it looked like they wouldn't find a vacant seat.

"I see one." Connor pointed toward a back corner of the room.

As Lanell slid into the booth across from him, the

equipment on her belt rattled, and the tang of his aftershave outranked the scent of frying meat and onions. He struck her as a cool, efficient person, probably an excellent pilot. Maybe she should book a flight with him. Now where had that silly thought come from?

He removed their sandwiches and drinks from the tray and slid it to the end of the table, sat and bowed his head for a moment, and then propped his forearm on the tabletop and studied her face for a moment. "Did you grow up around here?"

The question took her by surprise. And she didn't like airing her personal history. "No," she said briefly.

His mouth quirked. "City girl? Country girl? Or are you a butterfly who just happened to land in Springfield?"

So sure of himself. Persistent. And handsome. He would pester her until he had answers.

"I grew up in Kansas City."

"So how did you end up here?" He picked up his burger and began to unwrap it.

"After two years of junior college and waiting tables at a chain restaurant, I applied to three police academies. Springfield was the first to respond with an acceptance."

He tilted his head. "You did well, and have been a cop how long?"

"Three years."

He ran a measuring look over her. "So you're between twenty and twenty-five."

She rolled her eyes. "Twenty-four. Let's eat."

He took a big bite of his burger.

When they finished eating, he piled their wrappers

on the tray and returned his focus to her. "So what are your long range plans? Detective? Police chief?"

She grinned and shrugged. "Who knows?"

"Aah, the lady has lofty aspirations. I'm impressed."

She never expected to rise to the top spot, wasn't sure she would even want it. But she did want to move up in rank—and pay.

"What about your parents? Are they still in Kansas City?"

She stopped smiling. "My dad died in Iraq when I was two. My mother overdosed when I was eight. No relatives came forward to take me, so I grew up in foster care." And never felt truly loved or accepted. "Have you heard a lot of talk about our crime case?"

The sudden change of topic made him blink, but he caught up quickly, undoubtedly recognizing that he would get no more personal information. His smile resembled a smirk.

"I'm gone too much to hear local gossip, but I listen to the TV news when I'm home or in a motel. It doesn't sound like much progress is being made. Is that right?"

She grimaced. "Unfortunately, it's not moving as fast as everyone would like."

"How did the crooks get inside the building?"

"A window was broken, but evidence indicates it was done from the inside to make us think they entered through it." She didn't see any harm in telling him that much.

He nodded slowly. "So they wanted it to look like they got in on their own, but they had inside help, from someone with access to the room—or building. Do you have any idea who?"

"We're doing research on employees, checking backgrounds and police records," she said vaguely, reaching for her purse and exiting the booth.

On her way home, she stopped by the police station and posted a note in the work room about the high school athletic department's coat project. She stated that if anyone had coats to donate, they should hang them in Evan's office and she would pick them up every day or two.

Tuesday and Wednesday passed without incident, other than that it rained all day Tuesday, and the temperatures hovered just above the freezing mark, keeping people glued to their phones for weather reports. By Wednesday all precipitation had stopped, but clouds hung low over the city. A snow storm was predicted by the end of the week. The bright spot of the day was finding that half a dozen coats had been left at the police station for her to deliver to the school.

Chapter 6

Connor flew a group of tourists to Jamaica on Thursday. He would return for them Monday. When he arrived back at his home airport, he worked in the office for an hour and then headed to town. The clouds were low and gray, but the light snow that had been drifting down had stopped after lunch. Dampness penetrated with a cold bite.

The streets were busy, with festive decorations on light poles and in business windows. Christmas shoppers populated the sidewalks. He parked and joined the bustling crowd.

When he had found and bought gifts for his dad and sister, Dale, Justin, and their little ones, he made a beeline for the apartment. As he drove, the thoughts of Lanell that had plagued him all week returned to continue the malady.

Should he get her a Christmas gift? How would she react if he did? It was probably a good thing he hadn't.

He had to get a handle on his emotions regarding the woman.

He unlocked the door and pushed it open, hoping his dad had fixed something for supper. But the apartment was empty.

Connor hung his coat in the foyer closet and went to the kitchen, his stomach growling. He opened the refrigerator and pulled out the egg bin, a package of bacon, and some cheese. He had the bacon about cooked when he heard the front door slam.

"What are you fixing?" Steve asked when he entered the kitchen moments later. He peered at the counter. "Omelets?"

"Yeah." Connor couldn't work up much enthusiasm.

"How about I make some French toast to go with them?"

"Sure. Did you just get off work?"

Steve opened a cabinet door. "No, I came home, but then I ran down to the convenience store for some cigarettes."

Connor turned to face him. "I thought you had quit smoking."

His dad scowled. "I had, but I'm weak."

Connor scrutinized his face, the deepening lines that gave it a haggard look. A tinge of unease ran through him. "Are you feeling extra stress for some reason?"

Steve ran his tongue over his lips, as if his mouth was dry, and raked his fingers through his salt and pepper hair. "I got a letter from an old friend, and I have to make a decision."

The twinge of unease heightened. "Is it a tough one?"

Steve shrugged and pulled a flat bowl from the cabinet. "John has offered me a job. It's better than what I'm doing."

"So what's the problem?"

Steve paused in pouring milk over the two eggs he had just broken into the bowl. But then he added another dollop, placed the milk carton on the cabinet, and began stirring the mixture with a fork. "I wrote to John when I got out. He didn't need anyone then. Now he does. But it's in Colorado." He stirred harder, almost frantically.

Connor removed his skillet from the burner, stunned. "Can you think about it a while?"

Steve shook his head. "If I want the job, I have to grab it while it's available. It pays a lot better, and the work is steadier. I have to take it."

Now Connor was dealing with a dry mouth. "When do you have to leave?"

"In the morning," Steve said abruptly. He stopped stirring and faced Connor. "I appreciate you and Carly being here for me, but I need to take care of myself, and I can do that now."

Connor blinked, overcome with emotion. He was proud of his dad's attitude and desire to be self-sufficient, but he hated having him wrenched away so suddenly after already having lost so many years with him. "You know I want whatever's best for you—and so does Carly."

Steve nodded in short, jerky head motions. Then he put his arms around Connor. "I'm proud of you, Son." His voice was unsteady.

"We'll miss you," Connor managed to say.

As he started to crawl into bed that night, his phone rang. It was Dale. "Are you free tomorrow night?"

He thought of his schedule. "I should be home from work by six. What do you need?"

"We'll be working on our Christmas float, and

Coach Bergstrom just learned he has to attend a meeting out of town. The art teacher will oversee the students working on sign and banner lettering, and I'll work with the props and costumes group. I need someone to oversee the group constructing the framework."

"Where will you be working?"

"Jazzy Dwyer is letting us use her garage. Do you need directions?"

"Does she still live on Crandall?"

"Yes."

"I know where it is. What time are you gathering?"

"Six. But we'll take you whenever you can get there."

"I'll come straight there from work, and grab something to eat on the way."

"Won't your dad have supper waiting?"

He paused, his throat constricted. "He won't be home. He's leaving in the morning." He gave her a brief explanation.

"I hope it works out well for him."

Steve was packed to leave when Connor got up the next morning. They ate breakfast in solemn, near silence and parted in front of the apartment.

~

Lanell couldn't shake the feeling of unease she had about the older Mr. Prescott. He was a felon. He lived with his son and daughter, who had a close relationship with Dale Whitaker, who just happened to teach at the school where the murder had occurred. Dale had keys to a number of places at the school, including the storage buildings from which athletic equipment had been stolen. It wouldn't be all that hard to get hold of her key ring and make copies of keys.

She checked her email and found a message from Evan saying there had been another non-school robbery. Several items had been taken from the Super Sales Department Store and Pharmacy. With Steve Prescott already in her mind, Lanell couldn't help but wonder if he could be involved.

Pushing the troublesome thoughts aside, she left her office to patrol the grounds. An hour later she arrived at the cafeteria as the first lunch group was entering. She took up a post at the north wall.

When that group was gone, Dale entered ahead of her class. She stopped by the doorway and surveyed the room. When she spotted Lanell, she came to join her. "This should be the end of my duty assignments in here for this term," she said, sounding relieved. "Sometimes the extra duties are more tiring than teaching."

"You've been at it for how long now?"

"This is my fifteenth year."

Lanell grinned. "My, my, you're quite the veteran."

Dale smiled, and then her expression turned pensive. "What do you do when school is out for the summer?"

"I go back on the streets."

Dale gave an exaggerated, "Aaah. So you're a street walker, or cruiser, or …"

"Bum," Lanell supplied dryly. "What kind of bum are you in the summer?"

Dale chuckled, her dark eyes sparkling. "As many kinds of bum as I can get away with, which isn't too many with a husband and two little ones."

"You're a twin, right?"

"Yes. Derek is a conniving bum."

Lanell frowned. “He’s a rascal?”

Dale nodded. “He manipulated me into meeting his boss.”

Now Lanell laughed. “And you married the guy.”

“I did. He turned out to be a pretty nice fella. When he found out Connor and Carly’s situation, he stepped in and found help for them. So I had to marry him.”

“It sounds to me like Connor and Carly were very fortunate. They’re bound to appreciate the two of you.”

Dale placed two fingers between her teeth and emitted a short, sharp whistle. A finger pointed at two students who had begun some mild horseplay at their table. When the two jerked to attention, Dale returned her focus to Lanell. “We’re proud of both of them. Well, I’d better circulate,” she said, moving away.

Lanell continued her surveillance. When the cafeteria emptied, she made a salad from the salad bar and headed back to her office. As she passed the music room, sounds of the choir rehearsing for their Christmas concert grated on her. She wished she didn’t have to be on duty the night they presented it.

At the end of the day, she patrolled in front of the building as the students exited and hurried to their buses or cars. Thankfully the snow storm had not materialized. The temperature was close to forty degrees, with a fifty percent chance of rain tonight and clearing tomorrow. They would be working on the float inside a building tonight, so it would be fine. If the predictions held, there would be no rain on their parade tomorrow.

When the buses had caravanned out of the parking lot, Lanell circled the building and grounds, checking to be sure no one had been left behind and nothing was out of order. Seeing nothing awry, she entered the building, happy to be where it was dry and warm.

She was getting ready to go off duty when the superintendent called and reported that he thought someone had tried to get into the administrative offices. The secretary and bookkeeper had already left for the day, so he was alone in the building. He said he had heard sounds at the locked front door, but had seen no one around when he went to check.

"I'll be right there," Lanell said, zipping her coat and grabbing her hat from her desk.

She went out the rear exit and hurried up the hill to where the administrative building was located. The superintendent emerged through the doorway to meet her. He was a large man, with a shock of white hair and deep-set blue eyes.

"There are some scratches around the keyhole," he said, pointing at the knob.

Lanell examined it, and then faced him again. "The marks are barely visible, but it looks as if someone tried to jimmy it, maybe with a pocket knife."

He shook his head. "There are so many footprints in the snow that you can't deduce anything from them. We had a meeting up here this afternoon, and a lot of people were in and out. I should have left when everyone else did, but I stayed to make some phone calls and write a letter."

She saw no cars parked in front of the building. "Where's your car?"

"I parked in back to leave this space for those attending the meeting." He moved a hand in an arc that encompassed the limited parking area.

That meant that whoever had tried to gain access

had walked, and they couldn't be trailed in this tracked up mess. "I'll write up a report." She knew nothing more to do. He had to be of the same mind, but had called her so she would document it. They couldn't be too careful.

After returning to her office and writing the report, Lanell drove home and changed into comfortable street clothes, ate a snack of leftover chili, and listened to the TV news. The murder story was given another mention, with a brief interview of the superintendent. He had nothing to report, but assured parents and the public that the school was cooperating fully with the police and increasing security precautions at the campus.

Shortly before six, Lanell drove to the Dwyer home. The doors of a double garage were open, and—if she wasn't mistaken—that was Connor's SUV parked at the curb. More cars lined the street. A hay wagon was in the driveway, being pushed into one side of the garage by Connor, another male adult, and some students. Others milled about, anxious to get started. The opposite side of the garage was littered with big empty cardboard boxes and bags and boxes of supplies. Jazzy stood watch from one side of the driveway, obviously the commander-in-chief.

"Oh, hi," she said when Lanell approached her. "Glad you could join us."

Once the wagon was in place, the dark haired fellow with Connor came toward them. "Sorry I have to leave," he said to Jazzy. He had the same dark eyes and similar features as Dale.

"You've been a big help," Jazzy assured him.

He paused, his gaze locking in on Lanell. He extended a hand. "Hi, I'm Derek, Dale's handy brother.

And you are?"

"Lanell Rhodes. Dale doesn't know how unhandy I can be."

His face brightened. "Are you the cop who hangs out at the school?"

"That's me."

His smile was infectious. "It's nice to meet you. Wish I could stick around and get acquainted. But my wife thinks I should be present for our son's birthday party."

As he walked away, Jazzy went to the garage doors and gave a sharp whistle for attention. "All right," she addressed those assembled there. "The theme for this year's parade is Gifts of Christmas. We think we have a good idea for portraying that. Let's split the work into three groups. Mine will make all the signs and banners and do the lettering. We'll work in this front area so there will be better ventilation for our paint fumes. Mr. Prescott will oversee construction of the float bed, and Mrs. Whitaker's group will be in charge of props and costumes. They'll work in the back where it'll be less breezy for box wrapping." She pointed at the work bench in the rear of the garage.

The place was soon a buzz of activity. Although unheated, the enclosed garage was warmer than the outdoor thirty-five degree temperature, so they worked in their coats.

Lanell managed to stay busy without too much contact with Connor—but she observed him as he did a lot of the tool work. The mostly inexperienced workers, following his instructions, moved materials into place and held them while he anchored them. They built a partial deck in the back third of the wagon by fastening pallets to the bed. Then they put sheets of plywood over the pallet platform and built a wooden skirt frame that they covered with chicken wire.

Jazzy's group lettered the skirt framing, made banners, and decorated the chicken wire with a red floral background with white lettering that spelled *Gifts of Christmas*.

"There's a tree in the back of my van," Dale announced as her group finished wrapping the big cardboard boxes. "If someone will anchor it in place, we can decorate it."

By nine o'clock they had put the finishing touches to their masterpiece.

"Who's pulling this thing in the morning?" Connor asked.

"I figured I would," Dale answered. Lanell noted that her face was drawn and pale, her body moving as if so weary she had to force it.

Connor looked her over in a way that made Lanell think he was also concerned about his mentor's weary state. "Would you like me to do it?" he offered. "That way you could ride on the float with the students if you wish."

Dale seemed relieved. "Thanks. Coach Bergstrom was supposed to do it, but I was filling in because he'll be gone overnight."

"What time should I come get it?"

Jazzy spoke up. "The parade starts at ten. Participants are to line up at nine."

"I'll pick it up at eight-thirty then," he informed her. His attention shifted to Lanell. "Why don't you ride with me? I'll pick you up on my way here."

"It's the athletic department's float. I'm not a part

of them," she demurred.

"You work at the school," Dale said. "We'd love to have you on unofficial duty."

"See you in the morning," Connor said, sure she would not refuse Dale. He knew too much.

Lanell lingered until Connor and the students were gone. Then she helped Dale load her van. "You're beat," she said as they tucked bags of leftover materials in the back seat. "You're also troubled."

Dale jerked a shoulder. "There's a lot on my mind."

"School or personal?"

She was silent for several long moments. Then she blew out a gust of air. "It's my mom."

The admission punched Lanell in the gut. "Is she okay?"

Dale gazed into space over Lanell's shoulder. "I'm not sure."

"Care to explain?"

Dale gave her a weak smile. "I'm not sure I can. She talks about all her ailments and how serious they are, but then I'll catch sight of her getting around without her cane and …"

In other words, Dale also suspected her mother was faking. "I know it's none of my business, but I truly care. Ignore me if you don't want to answer, but I can't help but ask. What's the rest?"

Dale heaved a deep sigh. "She says she has no insurance and can't afford the expensive medicines she has to have."

"You're giving her money, and there's no end in sight."

Her lips tightened. "Yeah."

Lanell was not one to hug on people, but she put her arms around Dale's shoulders. "If there's anything I can do, will you let me know?"

Dale met her gaze in the glow of the street light. "There's nothing you can do, but thanks for the offer—and for caring."

The clang of the garage door dropping to the concrete brought them back to their current situation.

As they drove away in different directions, Lanell couldn't help but feel sympathy with Dale's plight. She couldn't deny the mother who had abandoned her, even knowing she was being used.

Chapter 7

Saturday morning was near freezing, but it wasn't snowing, and the sun could be seen trying to break through the gray clouds. The wind felt raw.

The rational part of Connor's mind told him he should steer clear of Lanell, but another part of him welcomed any opportunity to know her better. Anticipation of today's outing with her had him humming under his breath.

He drove to her apartment, saw her emerging from it, and pulled to the curb. She hurried to the SUV and crawled inside. She wore jeans and a heavy blue coat. "This feels good," she said, holding her bare hands before the warm air blowing from the heater. "We have to be crazy getting out in the cold on a day when we could be sleeping in, warm and cozy.

"You said it. I didn't." He pulled back into the street, drove to Jazzy's house, and backed up to her garage. Moments later the door began to rise.

The art teacher emerged, a huge bag in her arms. "I got the candy," she announced in her animated way. "I'd like to set it in your back seat rather than put it on the float."

Connor pushed a button to unlock the back door. "I

assume it's for students to toss to spectators as they ride through the street."

"Yep." She opened the door and dumped it inside. "It's Dale's and my contribution. Let's get you hitched."

Within minutes Connor had the float connected to the rear of his SUV, and they headed slowly down the street. Jazzy rode on the float to make sure nothing flew off of it in transit.

When they pulled into the field where the parade was to line up, it was already a bevy of activity. A parade coordinator trotted toward them, checking a clipboard in her hands. She pointed and yelled, "Pull over into that area."

As soon as Connor had parked, the coordinator walked to the driver's door and shoved a card toward him. "Here's your number. I'll let you know when to move into line." As soon as he took it, she walked away.

"It seems hectic and chaotic," Lanell commented, scanning the area.

"Everything will fall into place," Connor assured her. "That was Evelyn Jones, and she's a cracker jack organizer. It looks like students are beginning to locate us. Oh, and there's Dale," he added, spotting her in his rear view mirror. "She has a sack that I bet is more candy." He smacked his lips.

Lanell glared at him, but her eyes twinkled. "You look to me like a guy with a very sweet tooth. Don't you start snitching candy and make me have to arrest you."

"Yes, Ma'am." He stiffened his back and saluted.

She glanced behind them. "I'd better get Jazzy's

candy out there for her."

Connor laughed as she hopped out and took the bag from the back seat. He watched her take it to Dale, speak briefly, and then store their containers of sweets in opposite front corners of the float.

He exited the SUV and joined them. Dale waggled a finger at him. "Lanell has you pegged, Mr. Sweet Tooth. You two may as well wait in the vehicle while Jazzy and I get everyone ready and in position."

"Yes, Ma'am," he said in feigned meekness. He beckoned to Lanell. "Come on. If we're not wanted here, we may as well stay where we can keep warm."

They returned to the passenger seat and watched as local celebrities and dignitaries milled about, scout troops gathered, and a color guard assembled. The high school flag team was there, along with floats that represented churches, businesses, civic organizations, and more groups from the school.

Their own float held the big, wrapped boxes that bore labels of *Gift of Joy, Gift of Happiness, Gift of Peace, Gift of Love, Gift of Thankfulness,* and *Gift of Learning.* The students who stood in the boxes were dressed to portray toy soldiers, dolls, and a jack-in-the box. Jazzy was applying makeup to their faces, mostly red cheeks, while Dale helped them don and adjust wigs made of paper strings. Everyone seemed to be having a great time.

Connor looked over at Lanell. Sitting next to her in the quiet enclosed vehicle was comfortable—too comfortable. "Don't you have a sweet tooth?"

She shrugged, her eyes sparkling with mischief. "Not to the point of addiction, but I'd fight you for a milk chocolate brownie with nuts and milk chocolate frosting."

He laughed, and loved the sweet timbre of her laugh in return. "It's nice to find that a cop has a sense of humor."

"We aren't made of stone."

He let his gaze travel over her features one by one and come to rest on her mouth. "No, you're not," he said softly, reaching over and tracing his fingertips along the edge of her jaw and tucking a strand of hair behind her ear. When she didn't pull away, he moved robot-like closer to her. Their eyes met, and her pupils darkened. His head lowered, his heart thudding inside his chest. This was crazy, but he was about to kiss her.

The sudden shrill scream of a siren snapped the tenuous thread between them, and they sprang away from one another. He resumed his position behind the wheel and started the motor, hoping she didn't notice the trembling in his fingers.

They watched in silence as the fire truck pulled onto the street to lead the procession, the grand marshal and fire chief seated in the cab. The high school marching band marched in step along behind it, and then others followed in the order of the number on the cards they had been given. Evelyn moved about, signaling at them in turn.

The street was lined with people on both sides. As the parade rolled along, they scurried about picking up candy that was thrown from the floats.

When the parade finally wound into a parking lot that was its final destination to disband, Connor wasn't ready for it to end. Once parked, he and Lanell both exited the SUV and helped the teachers bag up the tree decorations and miscellaneous items they wanted to keep.

"Just pull the wagon into my drive and leave it," Jazzy instructed Connor when they were done and the students had all left. "I'll clean it off before Coach comes and gets it. Thanks for everything."

He pulled the wagon to Jazzy's house, unhitched it, and hopped back into the SUV. "It's eleven o'clock. Would you like to get something to eat?" he asked Lanell.

She frowned. "It sounds good, but I need to go home and take care of some neglected chores."

"Okay." He turned the key, disappointed, but not about to let her know how much. He started to pull into the street, but stopped when his cell phone rang. He considered ignoring it, but didn't when he saw that it was Carly. "What's up, Sis?"

"I think I need advice."

He tensed. "What's wrong?"

"Donna's in the hospital. Her husband beat her. When she regained consciousness, he was gone. She called me, and I went and got her and brought her here."

He had to think fast. She had to mean Donna Echols, whose husband and dad both were possible crooks. "Don't put yourself in danger," he cautioned.

"I'm safe here in the hospital. I've talked to Donna in bits and pieces when she was awake. She and Jack were fighting about money. She found out he stole from her dad. She can't tell her dad what Jack did because she's afraid he might kill Jack."

"What's her dad's name?"

"Lewis Clooney."

A light bulb flashed in his head. The man's name

had been in the news recently, linking him to an insurance scheme. Could he be part of the school theft ring? “What can I do?”

“I’m not sure,” she said, clearly upset. “I’m afraid to leave Donna. Her husband might show up and demand she be released and take her home with him. Like many abused women, she might go willingly. I can’t let him get his hands on her again.”

“Haven’t you called your department?”

“No, but I will.”

“Do it now, and be careful,” he repeated.

When they disconnected, he faced Lanell’s questioning look. “I think Carly’s uncertain how to handle a situation because of her personal involvement. Do you have time to listen?”

“Of course.”

While the motor idled, he repeated everything Carly had told him about Donna and her husband and dad. “I had an earlier conversation with Carly,” he continued when he had finished that. “Besides helping a wife who is being abused by her husband, my sister has another reason for befriending the woman.” He explained about the false accusation and firing of her friend. “She says Donna won’t report any abuse, and Heidi being fired isn’t a crime.”

~

Lanell’s mind reeled as Connor explained about his sister’s off duty investigation. “Jack Echols is known to the department. But this is the first I’ve heard of her friend’s plight. I wish Carly had confided in me, or someone. She can’t go the lone wolf route. Those guys are dangerous.”

“I think she’s realized that. She said she’s calling

the department now."

"Good. While she's doing that, you can drive me home, and I'll make a call." She reached for her phone and dialed Detective White.

When Lanell asked Evan about Clooney and Echols, he made a sound that was half groan, half pleasure. "I've been hoping to get something we can hang on those two, so I've already included them in my investigation. Jack Echols is a petty thief, not big time like our killer gang, and he was in jail during the time of the murder. I'll check on the father-in-law."

Connor seemed relieved when she disconnected and relayed Evan's report. She had just finished when he pulled up to her apartment building. She opened the door and hopped to the pavement. "I enjoyed it." She felt his gaze follow her as she turned and marched into the building.

As she took care of some overdue housekeeping, her mind constantly reverted to Connor. He was becoming a distraction, claiming her attention when she should be concentrating on other things, like getting her housework done, and doing some Christmas shopping.

His dad bothered her. Unable to shake her unease, she finally put away the vacuum cleaner and went to her computer. An hour later, that unease had increased. Steve Prescott fit the profile of their culprits. He was a felon. He had spent time with other violent offenders. And he could have gotten hold of Dale's keys and made copies. The discrepancy was that he had no history of any kind of burglary.

Monday evening Lanell kept her distance from where Dale Whitaker's family sat in the gym, but watched to see if Connor showed up to join them. She had about given up on him when he appeared just before half time of the first game. When the second half ended and the final buzzer sounded, she positioned herself by the doorway and waited for him to exit in the flow of people moving to the hallways. When he appeared, she followed him to the concession stand and held up a five dollar bill, pointed at him, and put up two fingers in a signal to the student behind the counter that she would pay for both their refreshments.

Sensing something, he spun around, and blinked in surprise.

"Don't say anything," she ordered. "This one's on me."

"That's not necessary," he said.

She placed the bill on the counter. "I know that. I want to do it. Now grab your drink before someone else does."

He laughed, shook his head in resignation, and did as ordered.

"Let's walk down the hall to some place quiet and private," she said when she had her own soda and change for her bill.

They strolled in the direction she indicated and turned a corner. At her office door, she pulled out her keys and unlocked it. "Let's step in here for a moment."

He looked puzzled, but did as she bid. Then he faced her. "Is this a tryst? Or do you have news for me?"

"No tryst," she said, her heart doing a weird thump-thump beat now that they were alone. "But I might have a little news. I just wanted to pass along to you that Evan says Echols has an airtight alibi for last Sunday night. Clooney owns several businesses and has a poor reputation, but he has no record. He also has an alibi for the time of Vernon's murder."

He scowled and sipped from his soda. "They're bad news. Too bad you can't get them off the streets."

"I wish we could," she agreed, sighing. "This has been a crazy week."

"What else has happened?"

"Yesterday the superintendent thought someone tried to break into the administrative offices," she said, not sure why she was bothering to tell him such a thing, other than it was a way to delay what she really wanted to talk to him about. "The lock had been picked at with something like a pocket knife, but the parking lot was empty and the snow too messed up from people attending a meeting an hour earlier to track anyone. I don't know what to think."

He took another sip from his soda. "You'll figure it out."

She cleared her throat, hating this. But she didn't want to have Evan question him. "I need to ask where your dad was last Sunday evening."

He froze, his expression turning thunderous. "You think he had something to do with those robberies? And Vernon's death?" Anger laced his rising voice. "If so, you also think I'm covering for him."

"I didn't say that. I just have to check everyth …"

"If you've investigated him," he cut her off, "as I'm sure you have if you're questioning me this way, you found that he's not a thief. He's just a poor working stiff who got in a fight, the other guy landed on the concrete and broke his neck, and Dad did time for it. Now, because he has a record, he's an automatic suspect for you? Well, forget it. And me." A cold mask fell over his face.

Sick at heart, Lanell shook her head. "Please understand my position."

He turned, back rigid, and stalked out of her office.

~

Connor couldn't sleep. He tossed and turned, going over and over his exit from Lanell's office and questioning the way he had lost it. Had he overreacted? Did he owe the woman an apology? The clock read well past midnight when he wearily made up his mind to confirm his dad's whereabouts during the critical time of the murder, and dispel Lanell's suspicions. He was working in the office all day tomorrow. He would take an extended lunch hour.

He woke bleary eyed and depressed. His morning work, fortunately, was routine enough that it didn't require an excess of brain power. His stomach rolling, he didn't bother to eat anything for lunch, but drove to the convenience store where Steve bought his cigarettes.

He pulled into the concrete drive and parked. Then he entered and approached the man in charge. "Do you know a man named Steve Prescott?"

The man's face crinkled in thought. "I don't know a last name, but there's a Steve who comes in a couple of times a week. He's a quiet fellow. Usually buys cigarettes and a candy bar."

"That sounds like him. Do you remember whether he was in here the Sunday evening after Thanksgiving?"

His expression turned distrustful. "Are you trying to cause trouble for the man?"

Connor shook his head and forced a smile, wanting

to put the guy at ease. “No, just the opposite. He’s my dad, and I need to verify that he could not have been somewhere specific that evening.”

The man hesitated, his mental wheels obviously turning. “Has someone tried to pin that school killing on him?”

Connor opted for full disclosure. “No, but I’ve been questioned. Dad has a record, and he had opportunity to access keys from a friend of mine.”

“If I’ve got the right Steve in mind,” the man said slowly, “he’s a nice guy, never causes any trouble. You got time to look at Sunday’s surveillance tape?”

“I’ll take time.”

“I’m Dick Moore, the manager,” he said, extending a handshake. Then he motioned for Connor to follow him.

Twenty minutes later, Connor emerged from the back room where he had watched enough tape to find Steve on it. The time stamped on it indicated Steve was in that store at 9:10.

“Thanks for everything,” he said to Dick. “I found what I needed. Do you mind not erasing that tape for a few days?”

“Sure,” the man agreed. “I’ll store it in a safe place. If anybody has to see it to believe you, tell ‘em to come ask for me personally.”

Connor drove back to the airport, but didn’t get out of his parked vehicle immediately. He composed a text and sent it to his dad, asking Steve if he was going to be able to come back to Springfield to spend Christmas with him and Carly.

Feeling better, he returned to work. When he left the airport late that afternoon, he drove to the school.

Only a couple of cars were still parked in front of it. He drove around the building and up the hill to the administrative offices, and was pleased to find no vehicles there.

Not sure what he hoped to find or learn—or even why he was there—he parked and exited the SUV. The walkways were clear, but the four inches of snow they had gotten earlier in the week was trampled and dirty, like Lanell had described.

He couldn't recall if she had said the superintendent's report had stated hearing an intruder only at the door, or if the windows had been checked. He left the sidewalk and studied the ground as he walked slowly to the end of the building and turned the corner.

As he did, he noticed some pinkish discoloration near the end of the small flower bed that fronted the building. He stopped and peered closer. Then he squatted to examine the spot more closely. The color didn't strike him as blood, his initial fear. Carefully, he probed a finger into the mushy snow and scraped it back.

He picked up a soggy roll of paper ammo.

Chapter 8

"That's the last of them," bus driver Kim Allman called cheerily Wednesday morning after releasing her load of students. She shut the bus door and drove across the parking lot.

Lanell turned to watch boys and girls file into the school building, and spotted Connor getting out of his SUV. Her muscles tautened. She wasn't ready for a confrontation. Maybe he would go on inside without seeing her.

He actually started to do that, but halted when he spotted her. He veered toward her. She waited, her gut churning. Had he come to let off steam?

His strong profile never failed to spike her admiration, as it did even now. She pasted a smile on her face and watched him approach. Sandy hair, an athletic build, there was a calm, capable air about him—and a guarded look in his piercing dark eyes. She knew he had overcome some incredible odds to become a man of strong character, one who could be a formidable adversary.

"Good morning," he said, his neutral tone revealing nothing.

"Morning," she returned, watching his hand reach

inside his coat and tug something from an inner pocket. He started to hand it to her, but hesitated. “Are you willing to talk to me after the way I acted yesterday?”

She relaxed a bit, realizing that he wasn’t here to give her a hard time. “Of course. Your reaction wasn’t unusual.”

“You were just doing your job, following procedure.”

“We’re both human. Let’s leave it at that. Okay?”

He nodded and extended his hand again. The item it held was a plastic bag with nothing more than a roll of narrow paper inside it. “Tell me what you think of this.”

She opened the bag and examined the reddish paper. It was damp. “Where did you get it?”

“I drove by here after work yesterday and walked around up at the administrative offices. I found that in the snow near the flower boxes at the side of the building.”

She looked at it again, recognizing ammo for toy pistols, but seeing no significance. “What do you make of it?”

His mouth moved in a way that indicated his tongue was sliding around inside it. “At the risk of meddling in your police case,” he said slowly, his eyes pinned on her face, “I think it means some young hooligans were snooping around up there.”

She considered the idea, remembering the details. “You don’t think there were any burglars, but just some kids prowling around. You could be right,” she allowed, meeting his gaze.

With a curt nod, he turned and started back to his vehicle.

"I'll check into it," she called after him.

He waved a hand in the air to acknowledge he had heard.

Lanell hung around the cafeteria while students ate breakfast. When classes had started and the halls were quiet, she went to her office and called the elementary principal.

When she had him on the line, she explained about the superintendent's alarm and what had been found near the building later. "Do you think some of your students could have been hanging around there?"

The phone went silent for several moments. "I think they could have been," he said at last.

"Do you have any idea why? Were they just loitering, or did they mean to vandalize?"

She could hear him heave a long breath. "This is just a guess, but I think they could have been looking for something. Yesterday I confiscated some cap pistols from two second graders and told them I was turning them over to an official. Our elementary students are released earlier than the high school. Those boys could have gone home—they don't live far from there—and ridden their bikes over to the offices."

Lanell had followed his account carefully. "Do you think they were peeking in to see if they could spot their weapons?"

"I'm afraid it's possible. Those two youngsters aren't typically troublemakers, but they're live wires. There's a disciplinary conference scheduled for tomorrow. Now they'll have to be questioned about this as well as the matter of bringing their guns to school. If they were snooping around up there, that will have to be added to the offenses to be evaluated. Their parents are not going to be happy."

He didn't sound happy either.

Lanell understood the man's position. With so many school shootings all over the country, there was heightened sensitivity about guns in school. Children had been disciplined for pointing their fingers like guns, for molding harmless materials into the shape of a gun, and other such actions. She was glad she didn't have to adjudicate this one.

Lanell thanked him for his input, disconnected, and left the office.

~

Connor had a west coast flight tomorrow and a layover, so it would be mid-morning Friday by the time he made it back to town. On his way home, he decided to stop by his boss's house for a chat. He wanted to see justice obtained for Vernon. Yes, the police—and Lanell—were working on it. But if there was anything he could contribute to the cause, he had an obligation to do it. He owed it to Vernon—and Carly.

"Come in," Dale Whitaker said when she opened the door in response to his knock. "I'm glad you stopped by. Or is it Justin you want to see?"

Connor stepped inside, pulling off his gloves, and nodded at his boss, who sat on the sofa with Jennifer cuddled up to him and Jax in his lap. "I don't want to intrude, but I'd like to run a couple of thoughts by the two of you."

"Have a seat, and I'll get us some drinks. Would you prefer coffee, tea, or hot chocolate?" She grinned, knowing how well he liked chocolate.

He chuckled. "As if you need to ask. That hot chocolate's just what I need to warm my insides."

He claimed a seat near Justin and extended an arm. “Would you like to unload one of those rascals?”

Before Justin could hand over the baby, Jennifer scrambled off the sofa and snuggled up next to him.

Dale returned and placed a mug on the table beside him and went to settle near her husband.

Connor picked it up and sipped, letting the hot sweetness warm him.

Dale leaned forward. “What’s on your mind?”

He took another sip and ignored Jennifer’s wiggling beside him. “I found something that may or not mean anything,” he began, and went on to explain about the superintendent’s report about hearing someone outside the administrative building—and later going by there and finding the paper ammo.

By the time he finished, Dale’s expression had become contemplative. “I haven’t been on the ball field in this freezing weather, but I recall seeing elementary age kids riding bikes around that area during softball season. In fact, there are some who ride regularly and sometimes stop by to watch us practice. They must live close by. I’m not sure how many get out in this cold, but I can see a couple of them venturing out under those circumstances. I think you should check with Lanell. She may have gained some more insight by now.”

He gave her a raised brow look. “You wouldn’t have ulterior motives, would you?”

She sat straighter, her expression one of exaggerated innocence. “I would never do anything so devious.” Then she became serious. “I’ve sensed something between you two.”

“She’s an attractive lady, and I assume a good resource officer, but there’s nothing personal between us."

"Is that a fact?" Her unblinking eyes pierced him.

"She has warned me away from police business."

"But you like her anyway."

"It'd be one-sided if I did."

Now she grinned. "I disagree. I saw a spark in her eyes. Shall I talk to her, point out your stellar qualities?" Her mouth twitched.

He glared. "I can do my own talking."

"Then do it."

On his way home, he considered what he should do next. Friday afternoon would be free, making a little longer weekend for him. By the time he arrived at the apartment, all he had done was decide to do some more scouting, and convinced himself that he should notify Lanell of his intentions.

With Dad gone and Carly on night duty, the place felt abandoned and lonely. He thawed a steak in the microwave, skillet grilled it, and fried some eggs and hash browns for a hasty supper. Then he took a shower and settled in front of the television.

After watching the weather report, he leaned back in the recliner and closed his eyes. A vision of Lanell's face swam behind his eyeballs.

Realizing he would find no escape, he sat up and grabbed his phone. Then he realized he didn't have her number. He thought a moment, and then dialed his boss. "I, uh, need something," he said when Justin answered.

"Spit it out," his boss ordered when he hesitated.

"A phone number," he blurted. "I need her phone number."

Silence. "By chance do you mean the school cop?"

Connor could have sworn he heard laughter in the man's head. "Yeah, that's the one," he growled.

"I'll have to ask Dale. Hang on."

Drat. He waited, hearing them speaking in the background. Then Dale came on the line and quoted the number in a carefully controlled voice.

"Thanks," he said briefly and disconnected.

He dialed the number.

"Hello."

"I have a little longer weekend, starting about noon Friday," he began without a greeting. "Dale says she has seen elementary age bikers in the area not far from the administrative building after school hours. I plan to spend some time watching that block Friday afternoon, and maybe talk to some kids if they come around. I just thought I'd let you know in case you want to monitor—or arrest—me."

"Don't hang up on me," she snapped, anticipating his next move.

A spurt of anger at her curt order was instantly overcome by a racing pulse. Confusion held him for a second, but then determination took over. "Vernon was a friend. There's a chance he would have become my brother-in-law. Don't tell me I can't be an observer or do anything to gain information that could help identify his killer."

"Cool down, Connor. The elementary principal confiscated some cap pistols from a couple of second graders, who may have been our prowlers. Meet me at the school at three-thirty Friday, and I'll monitor your stakeout."

He hauled a huge breath of relief. "I'll be there."

~

"Not much activity around here," Lanell observed Friday afternoon as Connor pulled to the curb where they would have a clear view of the school buildings and surrounding area. He had insisted on driving, and she didn't want to drive her cruiser that would draw attention. But she was still in uniform. He wore jeans and a heavy coat.

Sporadic light snow throughout the week had left slushy drifts against buildings and ditches. The sun was now intermittent, peeking from behind the clouds and disappearing again minutes later.

"You spoke too soon," Connor said as he parked.

Two young riders came into view down the sidewalk, so bundled up in coats and woolen hats and gloves that they looked like blobs on wheels. They veered into an open lot and stopped. One of them removed a plastic bag that had dangled from his bike's handlebars, laid the bike down, and took a football from the bag. His companion also deposited his bike. Together they walked onto the open lot and began to toss the football back and forth. Soon another biker joined them. And then another. They all looked to be anywhere from eight to twelve years old.

After watching them for a few minutes, Lanell looked over at Connor. "You ready to go talk to them?"

"You bet."

They met in front of the SUV and crossed the open area to approach the boys. "Time out," Lanell called, raising a palm high in the air.

The boy preparing to throw the ball stopped in mid-stride. He reminded Lanell of the Spanky character in the old Little Rascals films she had watched as a girl. The mother in one of the foster homes where she had stayed had owned a collection of them. All eyes turned on her and Connor, obviously alarmed at sight of her uniform.

"We need to talk to you, boys." She didn't want to frighten them, but letting them think they were in trouble might make them more forthcoming.

Their expressions remained wary. "We're not doing anything bad," the one with the football said, not moving from his position.

She softened her stance and expression. "I never said you are. I just need to ask you some questions—see if you can help us. Do you play here regularly?"

He studied her, his face tense with distrust. "Nobody's ever complained."

"I'm not complaining. I just want to know if you play here weekends."

He shrugged. "Sure."

She glanced at the other three boys, one at a time. They nodded. Good. "Were any of you here the Sunday evening after Thanksgiving?"

Now their expressions relaxed, becoming curious. Then *Spanky*'s face brightened with comprehension. "You mean when that teacher got killed, don't you?"

"That's right. Do any of you remember seeing any vehicles driving by or parking near that part of the school building?"

The four boys grew thoughtful, staring in that direction.

"We'd be most interested in any kind of truck you might have seen," Connor said, inserting himself into the conversation.

One of the boys, the one who reminded her of the Alfalfa rascal, minus the hair spike at the crown of his head, began to wag a finger in the air. "I remember something," he said, growing animated. "A white truck pulled in there and stopped just as we were leaving."

So no telling how long it had been there. Could it have been the thieves? They could have been there at that time. "Did you see the driver?"

The boy shook his head.

"I remember that truck," another boy said. "I didn't notice the driver, but I saw something on the side of the truck."

Lanell stepped nearer the boy, hope rising in her. "Tell me what you noticed."

His eyes darted to and fro, as if searching his memory. "It was a star. There was a name on the door, and the star was right over the top of it."

"Do you remember the name, or anything else about it?" She directed the question at all four boys.

Spanky shook his head. "I don't know models, but it was pretty old and dirty."

She looked back at the Alfalfa lookalike. "Was there more than one person in it?"

He frowned. "I'm not sure, but I think there might have been two. But maybe not. I wasn't paying attention. It was cold, and we had to get home."

She thought of a detail. "What color was the star?"

His face creased, and his eyes closed. "I think it was blue," he decided, opening his eyes after several moments. "I might be wrong, but it was dark, not yellow like a star should be."

"Thank you, boys. You've been a big help."

When she and Connor were back inside his SUV, she turned to face him. The giddy pleasure derived by the sight of him was not smart. Yet she found herself saying something stupid. "Would you consider being my unofficial, after hours, investigative sidekick?"

He ran his fingers back and forth over his upper lip, as if dealing with a tough decision. Then he grinned and extended the hand toward her. "It's a deal."

She placed her hand in his. Another mistake. The unexpected warmth that ran up her arm at his touch stole her breath. The look on his face told her he felt it too. Awareness sizzled between them.

She pulled her hand away. She shouldn't get personally involved with a guy whose dad was on her suspect list. She had to be sensible, stick to the case.

"I hate to rush you," she said, gathering her wits. "But I really need to get home and do some research."

He lifted an eyebrow, but started the vehicle.

Once she was alone in her apartment, Lanell called Detective White.

"Is that enough to give you any ideas?" she asked after relating her talk with the boys and hearing about the white truck. She waited when he didn't respond immediately, giving him time to think.

"The only company that comes to my mind with the word star in it is All Star Roofing," he said at last.

"I'm not on duty at school tomorrow since it's Saturday, so I can do some checking around if you'd like."

"I'd appreciate it. I'm supposed to be off, and my wife wants to Christmas shop."

When they disconnected, the deal she had made with Connor came to mind. She knew it was a mistake, but she had made him her unofficial sidekick. Now her conscience demanded that she invite him along.

Chapter 9

Connor was surprised when Lanell picked him up Saturday morning in uniform and driving a police car.

"I was called in this morning," she said as he slid into the passenger seat. "They're already shorthanded, and someone called in sick. Here, sign this."

He took the form she shoved in front of him. "Why?"

"I told the captain about our chat with those boys and what I had planned to do this morning. He said clock in and do it on paid time. But for you to ride with me, you have to release the department of liability in case of injury."

He signed and returned it. She tucked it in the glove compartment and put the car in motion. He stared straight ahead, trying to ignore her—and the pleasant floral scent that permeated the air around them.

"I made a list of garages on this side of town," she said as she looked both ways and pulled onto the highway.

They visited the garages nearest the school, and then branched out, asking managers and mechanics if they knew of such a truck. It was at the sixth place that they struck pay dirt. An owner recalled seeing an All Star Roofing Company truck that matched the description of the one they were seeking.

Connor's gut clutched at hearing the name of the company. He saw Lanell's eyes widen in reaction. She knew his dad had worked for a roofing company, and must suspect it was this one. He clamped his mouth shut, not about to broach the subject.

"It's owned by two brothers," the owner continued, wiping his hands on a grease rag. "Their last name is Hamilton. One's a little bitty guy they call Dinky. The other is a tall skinny guy named Rolly. We've worked on that truck a time or two. A guy by the name of Alvin who works for them is usually the one who brings it in when it needs anything."

"Can you tell us where to find it?" Lanell asked.

"The company's out in the northeastern part of town somewhere. Give me a minute and I'll look up the street address."

As soon as he handed over a scrap of paper on which he had scrawled it, they thanked him and set off to locate the place.

"It doesn't look like they're open," Connor observed as Lanell pulled into the lot of a rather shabby looking house that had been converted to a business headquarters. A sign on the building identified it as All Star Roofing on one line, with Roofing and Repairs beneath the name. The name of the owners was at the bottom. Parked about the property were a couple of trucks, a hot tar cooker, and assorted large equipment.

"It's Saturday," Lanell pointed out, pulling her phone from her pocket. She placed a call and asked for her captain. "There's no one at this All Star Roofing Company that we think owns that truck. Can you get me a home address for one or both of the owners? The names are Rolly and Dinky Hamilton."

She rummaged around in the glove compartment and pulled out a pad and pen while waiting. Then she wrote quickly. "Okay, let's find these guys," she said when she had the addresses. "It looks like they live next door to one another."

As they arrived at the block they were seeking and rolled slowly down the street, the radio crackled to life. There had been an attempted robbery at another school, and shooting had been involved. The two culprits had fled, and it was believed that one of them had been hit.

Connor studied the houses in the block. Then he pointed at the one where a truck was parked askew, partially in the driveway and partially on the lawn. "There's an All Star Roofing truck. Those attempted robbery guys could be the same ones we're hunting."

She pulled to the curb near the truck. "Stay here," she ordered, exiting the car and pulling her gun from its holster.

He wanted desperately to go with her, but he knew she was right. She didn't need a civilian in the way of police business. But he couldn't help but be afraid for her. While keeping his gaze locked on her, he prayed for her safety.

When he saw her yank the truck door open and lean inside, he changed his mind about not following her and was out of the car in two seconds. He ran up behind her, and looked over her shoulder to see a man slumped behind the wheel.

"He's been shot. Call 9 1 1," she said over her

shoulder while working over the man.

Reaching for his phone, Connor heard a low moan, but saw no chest movement that signified breathing. When a dispatcher responded, he told her a man had been shot and gave her the address.

"Help is on the way," he informed Lanell when he disconnected.

He watched her grip the man's wrist, checking for a pulse. "It's very faint," she said, glancing back at him. "I'm afraid to move him."

Connor peeled off his coat and held it toward her. "Put this over him."

She spread it over the motionless body and stepped back to face him. "He was taking low, gasping breaths when I first reached him. When I asked him who killed Vernon, he opened his eyes halfway and tried to answer, but I couldn't understand clearly what he said. It sounded like he might have said he's jinxed. Then he mumbled something else that sounded like 'Al got away,' but he was struggling to speak and mumbling so that I couldn't be absolutely sure. He closed his eyes again and went silent. He doesn't know who I am or where he is." She stopped speaking suddenly, as if just becoming aware that she was not speaking to another officer.

Shivering from the cold, Connor eyed the man slumped motionless behind the wheel, blood all over his hands—and surely on his torso beneath the coat he had handed to Lanell. He couldn't bear to think what it covered. "Do you think he's the would-be robber referred to in that radio call?"

She gave her head a jerky shake, as if chiding herself, and leaned back inside the truck. She reached behind the man and searched for a pocket. She pulled out a wallet, opened it, and found a drivers license. "It looks like his name is Marlin Tarkington."

"That's not the last name of the men who own that roofing company. He must be an employee."

They were silently debating possibilities when they heard the wail of an approaching siren. When the ambulance arrived, they stepped back to let the professionals do their work.

A police officer arrived moments later. He parked and approached them. "Is he still alive?"

Lanell grimaced. "Barely. It'll be a miracle if he makes it."

An EMT returned Connor's coat to him. "That was a good thing to do," he said, turning away. About frozen, Connor wasted no time getting back into it.

When the ambulance had left, siren screaming, Lanell faced Connor. "I have to go to the hospital, and then the police station. I'll drop you at your apartment on my way."

He would have liked to go along, but accepted that it would only cause problems for her. He went to the cruiser and got inside.

As he stepped back out of it in front of his apartment minutes later, he scolded himself. He found this woman so attractive it scared him. And he knew she suspected his dad of being involved in robbery and murder. The conflicting emotions were pulling him apart.

~

Lanell arrived at the hospital and learned that the gunshot victim had died enroute. She drove to the police station and went directly to her captain's office.

"Neither of the owners was at home," she began without preliminaries.

He leaned back in his desk chair. "I hate to put you off, but with being so shorthanded and Evan not here today, I'm going to have to follow up on this Monday." He sounded apologetic.

"I guess I'd better get back on the streets then," she said, struggling to restrain her frustration. "Is the officer who interrupted the robbery and shot the man okay?"

The captain nodded. "Fortunately, he was able to take cover and call for backup. He's safe physically, but pretty strung out emotionally."

She felt for Kip, but didn't have time to find and talk to him. "Can you get me some background on the dead man?"

"We can do that," the captain said, leaning forward.

"The driver's license in his wallet says his name is Marlin Tarkington." She laid it on his desk.

He wrote the name on his desk planner. "I'll contact you when I have something. I need you out in traffic now."

She hadn't been out there more than an hour when her phone announced a text.

She pulled into a restaurant parking lot to respond. It was from the captain.

Your victim went by nickname Tark. He's been known to use, and deal, drugs. He managed to finish high school, married, had a kid, and divorced. He's had a string of jobs, and lived with some woman who left him about a year ago.

Lanell assumed his drug use—and perhaps child support and alimony—had amounted to more than Tark made at the roofing company.

The rest of the day, thankfully, passed without any serious incidents. She was glad to get home where she could relax. Except she couldn't.

Vernon's unsolved murder weighed on her mind, and Connor's commitment to God and church haunted her. For so long she had avoided God and church. She wasn't sure quite what she believed, but she had never seen any justice for losing her parents the way she had—or for things like she had just witnessed. She had learned to be self-sufficient and didn't see that she needed God. Nor did she want to be fawned over or preached at by church people, however well intentioned.

Dale had invited her to church more than once, and Lanell sensed that Connor would like to invite her. The fact that he was sensible enough to not push helped make up her mind.

Sunday morning she walked into the church, and was looking around for a seat near the back when she saw Connor turn in an aisle seat to look behind him. His eyes lit with surprise when he spotted her, and he nodded a head signal for her to come sit with him.

Feeling eyes on her, she moved on down the aisle and slipped into the pew beside him. He leaned over and whispered, "I'm happy you're here." Then he helped her slip out of her coat.

Ill at ease, she brushed at the skirt of her dress and tried to focus on the service that was beginning. Being so close to Connor made it difficult.

When the service ended, she slipped into the aisle quickly, pulling her coat back over her shoulders. But Connor caught up with her and accompanied her out of the building.

Someone gripped her arm from behind. “It’s nice to have you with us this morning.”

Lanell turned and faced Jazzy Dwyer. She had known Jazzy in a casual way, but enjoyed getting to know her better when working on the Christmas float. “Thank you,” she said politely.

“We’d love to see you regularly,” the art teacher said, pushing the streak of black hair back from her face.

“I’ll think about it,” Lanell returned with a smile.

Jazzy waved and veered to the south section of the parking lot.

“I’m glad you came,” Connor repeated as they approached Lanell’s personal car, a Ford sedan. He started to say more, but didn’t, making her think he wanted to invite her to go to dinner with him. She was relieved when he didn’t. She needed to be alone and think.

The next morning was business as usual, except she couldn’t shake the ever-present thoughts of Connor and the emotional attachment she was developing for him. It had sneaked up on her, and she wasn’t sure what to do about it. Rationally she knew she should steer clear of him, while perversely wanting to know him better. It was a totally new—and uncomfortable—sensation. But she couldn’t let those feelings distract her from her job.

She had barely convinced herself she had her emotions under control when her phone rang. She picked it up from where she had laid it on her desk earlier. It was Detective White.

“What’s new?” she greeted him.

"The captain brought me up to date, and I've been out to that All Star Roofing Company. I managed to get a list of their employees, with addresses and phone numbers. I just emailed it to you."

Lanell grabbed her computer mouse and opened her email account. "It's here," she said, clicking to open it.

"I haven't had time to check them out yet, but I called the Better Business Bureau about the company," he continued, preventing her from focusing on the list yet. "They've had some problems with the IRS, but they seem to have a decent reputation regarding the quality of their work. But my gut says if they'll fudge on tax matters, they will on others."

As he spoke, Lanell let her gaze skim down the employee list on the screen, watching for the name of Connor's dad, half expecting to see it. Suddenly she stopped.

She must have made a startled sound, because Evan asked, "What is it?"

"Before he died, the guy who was shot in that attempted robbery said what sounded like 'Al got away'," she repeated slowly, closing her eyes for a few moments and visually reliving the scene. "The manager at the garage that identified the All Star truck said an Al usually drove it. There's an Alvin Jenkins on this list of employees."

Another thought suddenly occurred to her, but she didn't share that one. It was more coincidental, and the checking would have to be done here on school turf.

"I'll check on that name first," he said.

They agreed to keep in touch and disconnected.

Seeing it was almost time for the first batch of

students to arrive for lunch, Lanell headed for the cafeteria.

The room was almost full, with students seated at tables, and another group arriving, when a loud crash drew eyes to the line carrying their trays to a table. A tray had been dropped.

Lanell hurried to the student who had dropped it. The freshman girl's mouth trembled. "I'm sorry," she said unevenly. "I bumped Shirley's arm, and it slipped out of my hands."

"It's okay," Lanell assured her. "It was an accident. Go get another tray, and I'll find a janitor to clean up the mess."

Jazzy Dwyer came to the girl's side. "Go on, Jill. I'll stand here and see that no one steps in the mess while Miss Rhodes gets the janitor."

"Thanks," Lanell said, backing away. "Be right back."

She hurried to the office. "Will you page a janitor to the cafeteria?" she asked the secretary.

"Sure." Rose promptly pushed an intercom button and made the request.

Lanell returned to the cafeteria door and waited. It wasn't long until she spied Eddie coming up the hall, pushing his mop bucket.

"What happened?" he asked none too happily as he reached her.

Lanell explained. "Where's your pal?" she asked as she escorted him to where spaghetti had strewn in a wide swath on the floor. Jazzy returned to her seat.

"He's not here today," Eddie grumped. "He called in sick this morning. Said he has the flu."

As Lanell watched the students and staff eat, her

thoughts continued to swirl. The name Alvin Jenkins wouldn't leave her alone. Could that employee possibly be related to Claude?

When she finally had some time to slip into her office for a few minutes, she sat staring at the list of employee names Evan had sent, and decided to pay a visit to that business right after work. Then Connor returned to mind. Reminding herself that she had dubbed him her after hours sidekick, she texted him.

Can you meet me after school to visit that roofing company?

Minutes later she received a response.

I'll juggle some things. Meet you at the school at 3:45.

~

Connor griped the steering wheel in a stranglehold. He knew Lanell suspected his dad of involvement in the robbery and murder. And he was sure Steve was innocent. Yes, Dad had made mistakes, serious ones. And he had paid a huge price. But he had served his time, stayed out of trouble, and been released early for good behavior. Since then he had been attend church some and worked hard at the only job he had been able to find—until the Colorado offer.

He drew a cleansing breath and blew it out slowly, willing the tension in his body to ease. When this case began, Justin had sent him to check on Dale. After learning the severity of the situation, and its effect on Dale, Justin had said they would cover for him when necessary so he could stay abreast of the case and seize opportunities like this one. They all wanted Vernon's killer caught, and Connor wanted his dad cleared.

Buses were loading when he pulled into the school

parking lot. He found a spot among the student vehicles and waited for the lot to empty. When it had been vacated except for staff vehicles, Lanell raised a hand to signify she saw him, waved, and went inside the building. When she emerged ten minutes later, she beckoned for him to join her.

As soon as they were seated inside the police car, he signed her form and she started the motor. When they arrived at the roofing company, they found that the sign on the door said OPEN this time. She turned to face him across the seat. "I'll do the questioning. You just observe and remember what you see and hear."

He nodded. This was her mission, even if he did feel he had a stake in it.

Inside, the place wasn't much tidier than the outside. Paint was peeling from the walls, and the office, if you could call it that, was haphazard. The whole place could have benefited from some heavy use of a broom and mop. A man behind the counter was the only visible occupant.

When they approached the counter, Connor stayed slightly behind Lanell. The man eyed her a bit warily. He looked to be in his mid-thirties, with slicked-back brown hair, pale blue eyes, and a beak-like nose. "May I help you?" he asked in a raspy voice.

"Are you one of the owners of this place?" she asked.

He nodded. "I'm Rolly Hamilton. Are you here about Tark?"

She nodded slightly. "What can you tell us about him?"

The man shrugged and shook his head sadly. "He was a hard worker, but he liked his booze. I'm real sad about what happened to him. I can't figure out what he was doing in a robbery—if it really was one."

"Is Al working today?"

Lanell's question caused a bit of a startled reaction, but Rolly recovered quickly. He rubbed his bristly jaw. "He was, but he left early. Why? Is he in some kind of trouble?"

"I'm the officer who found Tark after he was shot," she explained briskly. "He was almost gone, but when I asked him a question, he said Al got away. The two were involved in a robbery and fled in separate vehicles. Tark was driving a company truck. We think Al got away in a different vehicle, maybe another of your trucks."

The man stepped back a pace, his eyes going wide. "That can't be. Both our trucks are locked in the big shed when we're not open."

"But some of your employees have keys, right?"

He shrugged. "Well, yes, but they wouldn't bother stuff when they're not on the clock."

"Where are they now?"

"Out on jobs with the other truck," he snapped angrily.

"Where's your brother?"

"Out checking on those jobs."

She leaned closer. "If we find out you're behind your hired hands' little weekend side jobs you'll answer for it. Consider yourself warned."

She spun and signaled with a head jerk for Connor to follow her back to the police car. Once inside, he noted the building behind the headquarters. "I guess that's where he means the trucks are kept."

She nodded, following his line of vision, her

expression grim. "I'd like to get a close up look at those company trucks, and inside every building here, but I don't have any proof that'll get a warrant."

Neither of them had anything to say as she drove back to the school. But when she pulled up next to his SUV and parked, Connor faced her. "You still think my dad's involved. He's not."

She opened the glove compartment and extracted a sheet of paper. "This is a list of that company's employees. He's not on it."

"Are you disappointed?" He couldn't keep the angry defensiveness from his voice.

She handed him the paper. "Look that over." She leaned back and waited, arms folded across her chest.

He hesitated, and then skimmed quickly. He had been certain that All Star was the name of the company where Steve had worked, but when his name didn't appear on the list, he decided to keep mum. Let her figure it out. He raised his chin a notch. "But you still think Dad is—was—involved."

"I didn't say that."

He gritted his teeth. Then the hostility suddenly drained from him. She wasn't vindicating, but she wasn't condemning. His mind went blank.

To his surprise, she reached over and placed a hand on his, jerking his benumbed mind back to attention.

His gaze pierced hers, and registered her pupils darkening. Then he committed the most stupid act of his life. He leaned over, pulled her to him, and kissed her soundly. His world tilted and spun, unfamiliar emotions coursing through him.

Then he released her, turned, and got out of there.

Chapter 10

Reeling, Lanell placed a hand over her mouth and sat frozen, her insides shaking as she watched Connor get in his vehicle and drive away. When he was gone, she darted her gaze over the entire parking lot and grounds, suddenly hoping that little scene had not been witnessed. She breathed a sigh of relief at seeing no one close enough to have noticed.

She slowly pulled herself together. Once she felt steady enough, she started the car and drove home. She pulled into her parking spot near her apartment and sat there, forcing her mind back onto the case. Then she called Evan.

"I'm not at my desk," he greeted her. "But I can give you one update. In the last school robbery, and we're assuming it's the same thieves who hit your school, they got away with a pile of photography equipment. I just left the school with a list of serial numbers. I'll send you a copy in the morning when I'm at my desk."

"You're making more progress than I am."

"I understand your need to be part of the investigation, but I'm responsible for the lead. What did you do that wasn't as productive as you wanted?"

They had worked together before she landed the school assignment, so he knew her well. “I went to that roofing company. We had been by there Saturday and found it closed.”

“Who’s we?”

She flinched, not anxious to involve Connor. “Do you remember the guy who showed up here at the school to check on Mrs. Whitaker after we found the body?”

“I sure do.”

If she wasn’t mistaken, there was a hint of amusement in his response. “He wants justice for Vernon Ziegler. The young man was mentored in high school by Mrs. Whitaker in a way similar to what she did for Connor and his sister. I’d like to ask you a couple of questions,” she continued hurriedly, before he could pursue the subject or end the call.

“Ask away, but make it quick. I’m headed to my car.”

She inhaled deeply. “I noticed an employee name on that roofing company list with the last name Jenkins. It’s probably just a coincidence, but I’d like to know if that person could possibly be related to a janitor who works at our school.”

“Give me the two names.”

“The one on the list is Alvin Jenkins. The school janitor is Claude Jenkins.”

“I’ll check in the morning.”

“Uh, one other name …if you don’t mind.”

“Another one on the list?”

“Uh, no,” she said uneasily.

“What’s the problem?” he asked after several moments.

"Well, Connor's dad worked for a roofing company before he left town, and I wondered …"

"If All Star is the one he worked for," he finished for her when she faltered. "What's the dad's name?"

"Steve Prescott," she said, feeling somehow that she was betraying Connor.

"I'll check," he said, and then added quickly, "There are a couple more coats in my office for you to collect. I've asked around, and it looks like this is the last bunch."

"Thanks for the way you've helped."

"Welcome. Maybe you need to send me an email with all your questions, so I don't forget anything or get the names confused."

"I will."

Lanell went inside her apartment and did just that. Then she spent a restless night, unable to erase that kiss from her mind. Right or wrong, Connor Prescott had invaded her life—and feelings. And it appeared he felt something for her as well. Facing that truth scared her witless.

She went to work the next morning tired and sleepy. Inside her office after classes had begun, she eyed the calendar on the wall. According to it, today was December seventeenth, only eight days until Christmas. School would dismiss right after lunch Friday for the holiday break and not resume until after New Year's Day. The prospect of the whole holiday thing failed to excite her. But since she would be on regular patrol duty or working in the office during that time, she could concentrate on the murder case during normal work day hours.

When she checked her email and found Evan's list

of stolen photographic equipment, she printed a copy and stuck it in her purse. In the body of the message he stated that Alvin Jenkins was indeed a brother to Claude, and that Steve Prescott had been employed at All Star Roofing.

During lunch Lanell approached the table where the school's photography teacher sat. She leaned over and spoke softly into Leland's ear. "I think you should take extra precautions with your lab. Photography equipment was taken in the last school heist."

He nodded, putting his fork down. "I can't imagine those burglars would have the nerve to hit us again, but I'll practice tighter security measures. Thanks for the warning."

After school, Lanell made a final round of the buildings, checking locks and making sure everything was secure. Then she took her time before leaving. Not wanting to eat out, she drove straight home. She was foraging in the refrigerator for something to eat when a knock sounded at the door.

Not happy about being disturbed, she closed the refrigerator and plodded to the door. She found Connor standing on her doorstep, a bouquet of flowers in his hand.

~

Connor swallowed nervously and shoved the flowers at Lanell. His heart thumped so loud and erratically he feared she could hear it.

Her mouth did a funny little movement as she took his floral offering.

"What happened yesterday shouldn't have," he blurted. "I hope you're not mad at me."

She stared down at the flowers, and then looked at

him. “It wasn’t about us. It was stress over finding Vernon’s killer.”

“Uh, I have some Mexican takeout in my bus-mobile, if you’d care for something to eat,” he said awkwardly.

“Oh, get it and come on in here,” she said, a hint of amusement in her tone and expression.

Relieved, he turned and sprinted to his SUV. He grabbed the food containers and practically skated back to the house and through the doorway. She was placing the flowers on the coffee table. When she turned around, he handed her the food. “I’m hungry,” he said inanely, deciding it would be prudent to not mention yesterday again.

She pushed a strand of stray blond hair away from her cheek.

“Shall I make coffee, or would you prefer tea, or a soda?”

“Whatever you’re having is fine. I like all of them.”

They ended up with iced tea and a meal that grew more comfortable as it progressed.

Lanell wiped her mouth and put the napkin down. “How did you know I love tacos?”

He grinned. “I’m psychic. Or maybe I just think because I love them that everyone else does. Carly likes them, but she prefers tostados and taco salad.”

At mention of Carly’s name, Lanell’s face took on a pensive, almost solemn, look. She placed her forearms on the table and gazed over at him, her posture tense. “I work for the same department as your sister, but I hardly know her.”

Connor suspected he knew what was troubling her.

"You've noticed something that bothers you, and you're not sure if it's okay to ask."

She nodded. "More than once I've seen her with someone who may not be trustworthy."

"Carly's straight," he said, wanting her to understand. "You've seen her with Donna Echols." He shared what Carly had told him about Donna's abusive marriage and wanting to find justice for her friend who had been unjustly fired.

Lanell's expression had gradually softened as he explained. "I'm not sure I condone her lone wolf approach, but I guess she doesn't think there's enough proof of wrongdoing to make clearing her friend's name a formal charge."

"There's that, but I think it's also the friend's wishes she's honoring. As for the lone wolf method, Carly has always marched a little too much to her own drummer."

Now Lanell grinned. "She must have followed the lead of her big brother."

"She might in some ways, but not in either of her choices of career."

Crinkles formed across her brow. "What was her other one?"

"She breezed through beauty school right after high school, and went to work in a local shop. She became caught up in the problems of her clients, and eventually decided that she could accomplish more for them as a cop than as a hairdresser. Among other things, she's involved with a women's shelter. I wish you could become friends with her, maybe give her some advice."

"I won't force myself on her," Lanell said thoughtfully, "but I'd welcome a friendly relationship with her."

That was good enough. "You might want to tread lightly on the subject of our murder case."

Her eyes clouded. "You're right. She probably wants to get directly involved in finding her boyfriend's killer, but she's not assigned to the case. I hope she's not trying on her own."

Like he was? It was out of his hands.

"There's something else I'd like to say while we're on the subject of my family."

She went still, her eyes boring into him.

He took a deep breath. "After you implied that Dad could be involved in the burglaries, I checked on his whereabouts the Sunday evening Vernon was killed. There's a convenience store not far from our apartment where he buys cigarettes and snacks. The manager confirmed that Dad was in there that evening. He has it on surveillance tape."

She nodded slowly. "I hope you realize I'm just trying to do my job. It sounds like you've done it for me."

He nodded. "I understand your position, but I have to look after my dad. He's been through too much to end up back in prison for something he hasn't done."

"I get that," she said softly. "I'm glad you found proof. If you'll tell me which convenience store, I'll pick up that tape. But right now I have to go be on duty during the high school choir concert."

~

"Are you doing anything tonight?" Dale Whitaker asked, approaching Lanell at the north cafeteria wall during lunch duty the next day.

She wasn't, but Lanell was suspicious and hesitant

to open herself to anything she didn't want to do. "What are you doing?" she asked.

Dale grinned. "Our church Christmas program is tonight. If you're not busy, we'd love to have you come. Jennifer will be in it for the first time."

That was cheating. Dale knew she couldn't resist the little girl. "I'll think about it," was all she promised. But she knew she would go. If she could get through last night's choir concert—which hadn't been as difficult as she had expected—she reasoned that she could surely get through a church program

"Think real hard," Dale ordered, grinning as she headed back to her lunch table.

After school, Lanell drove to the police station. To her surprise, Carly was at her locker, her back to the doorway. As Lanell opened her own locker door, Carly turned. "Oh, hi," she said, startled.

"Are you just coming on duty?" Lanell asked.

"Pretty soon," Carly said, holstering the gun she had taken from her locker. "I was restless and came in early. I need a cup of coffee before facing the cold."

"Do you mind if I join you?"

She shrugged. "It's a free world—and the coffee's good." Now she grinned.

Together they went to the little room that served as a lounge/work room, took the mugs with their names labeled on them from a shelf, and filled them from the pot the office staff took turns making. They each tossed some change into the bowl that held money used to purchase the stuff and sat across from one another at the long table in the center of the room.

Lanell felt suddenly helpless, unsure how to express herself. "Carly, I'm so sorry about Vernon. I wish there was something I could do for you."

"Find his killer," Carly said tightly, and then bit her lips to control their trembling.

Lanell reached over, gave her hand a squeeze, and released it. "Evan and I plan to do just that. I didn't know Vernon well, but he seemed like a real nice guy."

"He was. I know he's in heaven, but I miss him." Her words had grown softer as she spoke.

Lanell's throat thickened with emotion. "I sense that you're strong, like him and your brother. You'll at least have positive memories of him."

Carly nodded and blinked back tears, her fist clenched. "I wish I could get my hands on the scumbag who did it. Will you tell me where you and Evan are in the investigation?"

Welcoming the interaction, Lanell went over what they had so far done and learned. "Rolly Hamilton said his brother was out checking on their jobs while he worked in the office," she said after describing her and Connor's visit to the roofing company. "What I'm wondering is if the brother is actually part of the burglary ring, and if he was there when Vernon was killed. The guy who died after the last interrupted burglary said 'Al got away,' so there were at least two involved in that job. I think there were two in our case."

"At least two," Carly agreed, having taken it all in attentively. "Do you have any idea who Al is?"

"Evan is checking employee lists," she hedged, not ready to air her suspicions about the janitor yet. Feeling somewhat cowardly, she changed the subject. "After I found out your brother's connection to you, I mentioned seeing you with Donna Echols."

"And you didn't think much of it," Carly

responded, a bit tartly.

Lanell flinched inwardly, but kept her expression calm. "It's not my business to judge your relationship, but I did hope you were aware of certain facts."

Carly eyed her intently, almost belligerently, and then seemed to deflate. "I suppose he explained my purpose." It was inflected as a question.

"He told me you're trying to help Donna, and that you're also looking for a way to clear a friend's name and work record."

Carly expelled a weary sigh. "Yeah, well, I'm not having a lot of success. Donna wants to leave her husband—and dad."

"Is there anything I can do? I'll be back on patrol during the school's holiday break. It starts after lunch Friday."

A spark of new interest entered Carly's eyes. "Connor could fly her wherever she needed to go if she can work up the nerve to leave," she said slowly, thinking out loud. Then she started and glanced at her watch. "I've got to get moving," she said, getting to her feet. "I'll talk to Donna and see if she's ready to quit waffling and get away from Jack."

When she was gone, Lanell drained her coffee and went to a departmental computer. She spent the next hour researching all the background she could find on Leona Denning and Claude and Alvin Jenkins. It took some digging, but what she found was a history of petty schemes that heightened her concerns about Dale.

After sending a copy of her findings to Evan, who was off duty today, Lanell headed home. It was raining, with the temperature dropping fast. As she drove, she remembered Dale's invitation for tonight. She didn't really want to go to a Christmas program, but Dale seemed to be reaching out to her for support.

When she entered the church an hour later, the lights had already been dimmed in the sanctuary. Stage lights at the front focused on a nativity scene that had been created on the stage.

Lanell slipped into a pew near the back. As she sat waiting for the program to begin, the sight of the crude cradle on the stage brought back memories. There had been a time in her childhood when she and her parents had attended church and sought God's guidance. When she was five she had been an angel in a scene similar to this one. It had been a thrilling experience.

How had life changed so much?

After her dad's death, her mother had fallen into a deep depression, and then turned to drugs. Lanell had continued attending church with the family of a neighborhood friend. But after her mother died and she was placed in foster care, she had no longer felt that God cared about her.

Now, staring at that nativity scene, her heart yearned for that childlike fervor and belief. She thought of the people she saw every day, and it came to her how much happier demeanors the ones who lived Christian lives wore, and the stronger coping skills they exhibited.

God, do You really care about me?

As a sensation of warm comfort settled over her, there was motion in the aisle next to her. She looked around, and Connor squeezed into the small space between her and the end of the pew. She scooted over.

"Fancy seeing you here," he whispered into her ear.

"Dale invited me," she whispered back. Then they both went quiet as the program began.

When the angels appeared, Jennifer Whitaker waved at her parents, causing a stir of amusement among the spectators. She and Connor exchanged amused glances. "She's a ham," he whispered. She nodded.

In a pew near the front, Lanell spotted Dale and Justin. Dale's mother and Claude sat to the left of them in the same pew.

Lanell hated the negative vibes that washed through her. She returned her attention to the narration and enactment of the Christmas story.

"That was cute," Connor said as the youngsters exited the stage.

Lanell nodded agreement, stood, and picked up her coat.

"There'll be refreshments in the fellowship hall," he said. "Can you stay?"

She thought longingly of sleep, but a snack sounded good. "Okay."

As they joined the flow of people heading toward a doorway at the south side of the sanctuary, Lanell gave him a quick account of her chat with Carly. "She wants to help Donna get away from her abusive husband. Can you provide transportation if she wants to leave the area?"

"I can, but I'll need a little notice to fit it into my work schedule when I'm not on a flight. Carly works with a women's shelter. You could take her there and contact me when you have a destination in mind for her."

After meeting and greeting a number of church

members, they joined Dale's group that now included her twin brother and his wife and two-year-old son. They spent a pleasant half hour chatting and enjoying punch and snack goodies. Lanell was glad when Dale announced that it was bedtime for her little ones and prepared to leave. Leona and Claude followed close after Dale and her family, with Derek and his wife and baby behind them. Lanell and Connor brought up the rear.

All during the reception Lanell had watched Dale's mother, noting how she leaned heavily on her cane and acted sickly in a way that struck her as less than genuine. She hated feeling that way, but couldn't prevent her misgivings.

When they exited the building, the temperature had dropped low enough to make the rain form an icy slush on the porch and steps. A few drops of icy liquid blew into the faces of people as they hurried to their cars. Lanell pulled the hood of her coat up further.

Suddenly Leona gasped and stumbled. Flailing, she clutched Claude's arm and sank into a heap on the concrete surface, pulling him down with her.

Chapter 11

Connor started forward to help with the fallen couple, but paused when Derek beat him to the scene.

"Should I call an ambulance?' he asked Dale, who stood bent over her mother's form while Derek held the woman steady.

"Yes," she called over her shoulder.

"No," the mother yelped, raising her head, and then lowering it. "No insurance," she said in a pitiful moan.

Dale waved at him to go ahead, while assuring her mother that she would take care of it.

Connor pulled his phone from his pocket to dial, but had to wipe icy drops from the screen. When a voice responded, he stated the need and location. "They're on the way," he reported when he disconnected.

He went to where Justin was assisting Claude to his feet. "Let me help." He leaned over and took the opposite arm from the one Justin was gripping.

The bony man reached up and clasped the extended hand. "Thanks," he said when they boosted him upright. He rubbed a hand up and down his backside.

By now Leona had been eased to a sitting position, but Dale told her to sit still and try to relax her muscles.

Within five minutes the ambulance arrived, and two EMT's emerged. They hustled to the rear of the vehicle, removed a gurney, and began to maneuver it up the steps. One medic tugged at it from the front while the other pushed at the back, ignoring the icy rain pelting them.

Everyone kept out of their way, but once they were on level surface, Claude stepped toward them, and his feet slipped on the ice. Arms flailing, he lunged toward the gurney and crashed into it, sending it ker-thumping back down the steps.

Connor grabbed the man's arm to steady him while the medics retrieved the gurney. Without comment they parked it at the bottom of the steps and came on up without it, lifted Leona, and carried her down the steps and strapped her on it. The whole scene seemed bizarre.

As they loaded the woman into the ambulance and allowed Dale to accompany her, Connor darted a sideways glance at Lanell. She seemed disturbed.

When the ambulance rolled away, Justin's car following with Claude inside, the remaining spectators went on to their cars. Connor faced Lanell. "Are you thinking what I'm thinking?"

She grimaced. "Maybe, but I'm not certain enough to say it."

He took her arm. "Let's get in your car and talk."

She didn't object as he escorted her to the sedan, walking easier now that the precipitation had come to a near stop. When she unlocked the doors and got behind the wheel, he went around to the passenger seat.

He cut to the chase. "What are your feelings about Dale's mother?"

She tipped her head, studying him in the dome light. "I've not been getting good vibes," she admitted at last.

"You're not the only one who has suspicions," he said, unsure how to proceed, but feeling compelled to share what he knew.

Her gaze didn't waver. "Are you thinking the lady

is exaggerating her health problems as a way to *guilt* Dale and Derek into forking over money?"

He inhaled heavily. "Justin thinks that's what's happening. He shared his concern with me after Dale gave her more money to have prescriptions filled."

Lanell's face hardened. "When was that?"

"A couple of days ago."

"Do you have any idea what doctor or pharmacy she's supposed to be using?"

He rubbed his jaw, trying to remember if any specific ones had been mentioned. "I think Justin mentioned Leona saying she couldn't get her medicines from Walgreens because she didn't have the money. I don't think she meant to end up in the hospital tonight. I think she just wanted to garner sympathy, and in this case wangle money for a doctor that wouldn't happen."

Lanell nodded. "I'll check the pharmacies in the area and see if she has filled any prescriptions with that money."

Relief flooded him. "Thanks. I've been concerned, and couldn't think of anything I could do about it. I'd better let you go so you can get out of this weather."

~

Lanell woke Thursday morning before the alarm sounded. She sat up in the bed and peeked behind the curtains to see that hardly any ice from last night's brief spate of sleet covered the ground. Having had no school cancellation call, she turned on the TV weather report and heard a forecast of more inclement weather, but it was not expected to arrive until the weekend. It looked like they would make it to the holiday break without missing any school days.

She ate a bowl of cereal, dressed, and went to work. She had delivered the last batch of coats to Dale, overseen student arrivals, and was back inside the building when Claude came ambling down the hall, pushing a cart of supplies.

"How are you feeling?" she asked as he passed within a few feet of her.

He stopped and looked back. "My hip's a little sore, but I'm okay."

"How's Leona?"

"She was dehydrated, and her blood pressure was low. Soon as they get it regulated, the doctor said she can come home."

Lanell couldn't help but think how easy it would be to manipulate such a condition. "Thanks for the update." She was tempted to ask him about his brother, Alvin, but resisted.

He resumed his trek down the hall.

The rest of the day passed peacefully. But Friday morning the halls vibrated with a sense of excitement and expectancy, students and staff anxious to be free for the next several days. After school dismissed early, she didn't linger, but drove to the nearest Walgreens and asked the pharmacist if any prescriptions had been filled for Leona recently. They had not.

She checked every location in the city directory, with the same results. If any prescriptions were being filled, it wasn't at Walgreens.

Tired, hungry, and irritated, Lanell sat in her cruiser before heading home. she pulled out her phone to call Connor, but before she could dial, it rang. It was Carly.

"Lanell, I'm on duty, and Donna just called. Things have been so bad between her and Jack lately that she's been working on an escape plan, keeping her car gassed up, and hiding some emergency cash, clothes, and documents for a fast getaway."

"I take it that time has come," she said when Carly paused for a breath.

"Yes. She just called and said he held a gun to her

head and told her he was going to kill her and then himself. He didn't, but she's afraid he will next time. While he was in the shower, she grabbed her hidden suitcase and drove to a grocery store not far from you. Can you possibly go meet her and take her to the women's shelter where the woman in charge has already been alerted to expect her?"

Carly obviously thought Lanell was already home from work. She didn't bother to enlighten her. "Tell me where to find her, and the address of the shelter."

As soon as she had the information, she hit the streets. At the grocery store, she found Donna in the canned goods section, where Carly had said to look for her. The tousle-headed woman had a shopping cart parked in front of her, and was staring at a can label as if reading it.

Lanell turned into the aisle and walked up next to her. "Carly sent me," she said quietly. "Go get in your car. I'm driving a police cruiser. When I pull out, follow me."

Donna nodded, but didn't speak. Her solemn face was etched with lines of stress, her blue eyes darting about fearfully. She put down the can and, leaving her cart behind, headed for the front of the store.

As Lanell followed the woman out to the parking lot, she considered God's role in all this. Did He care about people who were hurting? Connor's face floated into her mind. He would say yes. He had a faith she didn't. He would ask God's guidance. Instilled with a new confidence, she silently prayed that God would control this situation.

She watched Donna get into a dark blue Ford car. Then she hurried to her marked car and drove past her out of the parking lot.

With the blue Ford behind her, Lanell drove to the address Carly had given her and parked at the curb.

When Donna parked behind her, Lanell got out and waited near her cruiser as Donna exited and took a suitcase from the back seat.

"I'm sure they'll tell you these things," she said as they walked to the front steps of the big, older house, "but I'll go over them anyhow. Get an unlisted phone number and cancel your old bank and credit card accounts. When you open a new account, use a different bank, and when you get relocated, apply to the address confidentiality program, a service that will confidentially forward your mail for you."

"Thank you," Donna said as they went up the steps. "Carly has been wonderful, and now you're the same."

Lanell rang the bell, and an older, gray haired lady opened the door. "Come in," she said. "Carly called, so we were expecting you." She shifted her attention to Donna. "Give me your car keys, and I'll have someone park it where it can't be seen."

Lanell faced Donna. "You're in good hands now. I'll head on home. I'm glad I was available when Carly called."

She waited until she pulled up at her apartment to call Carly. "She's safe now."

They chatted for a couple of minutes. After they disconnected, Lanell called Connor. "Two things," she said as soon as he answered. She explained about meeting Donna for Carly. Then she paused.

"What's the second thing?" he prompted, as if sensing her unease.

"Before Carly called about Donna, I visited the Walgreen pharmacies," she said tautly. "None of them had any records of prescriptions for Leona."

"She's pocketing the money," he said in weary resignation. "I'll tell Justin, and he'll have to decide whether to discuss it with Dale."

He thanked her for the information and they ended

the call.

Tired and hungry, Lanell entered her apartment and made herself an egg sandwich. She had just sat down to eat it when her phone rang.

With a growl of frustration, she dashed to the living room to get it from her purse. It was Evan. "What now?" she said somewhat ungraciously.

"The lady bear sounds tired. I won't keep you. I just have a quick update I thought you might like to hear. There was another convenience store robbery this afternoon. Jack Echols has been arrested. With the string of arrests he already has, this may put him away for a long time."

Lanell thanked him and returned to her sandwich. Maybe Donna wouldn't have to leave town after all.

~

Connor left the cockpit and flexed his muscles, happy to be on his feet. He'd left Springfield that morning, flown a shipment of emergency supplies to a company in Idaho, and then circled around here to Denver. He caught a taxi and had it take him to the address his dad had given him a few days after coming out here.

The Saturday afternoon temperature was almost freezing, and clouds hung low in the west. But there had been no snow here today, and the forecast called for rising temperatures tomorrow.

He had other concerns, though. A jumble of disjointed thoughts and facts pecked at his brain, making it hard for him to concentrate on business.

Lanell was right. The murder investigation was the job of the police, and they knew how to do it. Yet his thoughts constantly reverted to the case, and his desire to see justice for Vernon. But right now he needed to further the relationship he had begun with his dad.

He had called last night to be sure Steve wouldn't be working today and he could stop by. He knocked at the door.

Steve squinted at him in the doorway, rubbing a hand over his lightly whiskered face. "I fell asleep on the couch. Come on inside."

The sparsely furnished apartment smelled of coffee. Connor inhaled with a sniff. "Got any fresh?"

"I can have in a jiffy. Can you stay for supper? I've got some nice steaks."

It was only three o'clock, and tomorrow being Sunday meant he had no set time to be home tonight. "That sounds good."

Connor followed his dad into the small kitchen and leaned against the counter, arms folded across his chest, while Steve made the coffee. When he had it brewing, they sat at the small round table to drink it.

"How's the new job going?"

"Pretty good," Steve allowed, shrugging. "I'm a good roofer and carpenter, if I say so myself. But I seem to be turning into a floor installer. That's what John needed, and I do what's needed."

"Tell me about John. You said he's a friend, right?"

Steve ran a work roughened hand through his already rumpled hair. "Yeah, we worked together back before I …got in trouble. A couple of years ago he came out here to join his brother and start their own company."

They chatted for a while, and then Steve stood. "I'll put the steaks on now. You want to wash some spuds and put them in the oven?"

It felt good to work together over the simple tasks of fixing a meal.

"I'm glad things are going better for you," Connor said when they were finished eating.

Steve sipped from his coffee mug and put it down.

"I don't know that I'm doing all that much better, assuming you meant financial. But I'm sure more relaxed."

Connor hunched forward, his arms on the edge of the table. "What do you mean?"

A parade of emotions shadowed his dad's features. "I hated leaving you and Carly. We were just getting reacquainted. But I wasn't real comfortable with that outfit I was working for."

He focused on Steve's expression, studying every nuance. "How much do you know about them?"

His dad traced invisible circles on the table with an index finger. "I only met the Hamilton brothers when I went to work there, and I only stayed a few months, so I didn't get to know them real well. They seemed to have a lot of connections around the area and beyond. I suppose that was good, but something about them made me uneasy. They spent a lot of time on their phones, and I'm afraid they didn't always treat their customers right. I have no proof of anything, mind you, but something about the whole operation just didn't smell right."

"Your instincts were correct."

Steve jerked back, and his finger went still. "Has something happened?"

"Do you remember employees by the names of Tark and Alvin?"

"Of course I do." He leaned forward farther, frowning.

If Connor had not already been convinced of his dad's innocence, he certainly was now. Steve was clearly baffled.

"You know there's been a rash of burglaries at the area schools," he said, and went on to explain how he and Lanell had been led to All Star Roofing.

"I like that Dale," Steve interjected when her name was mentioned. "She was good to you and Carly. I owe her."

"So do Carly and I. There was another school robbery recently, and one of the burglars was shot. He died."

Steve drew in a sharp breath. "Are you saying it was one of those guys?"

Connor nodded.

"Which one?" he demanded, his posture gone rigid.

Connor cleared his throat. "Lanell found Tark in his truck. Before he died, he said what sounded like 'Al got away'.'"

"So Tark's dead, and Al's on the run?"

Connor nodded again.

Steve sat in silent contemplation for several long moments. "Are the Hamilton brothers behind this stuff, or are the employees operating on their own?"

"Nothing's been proven yet. Do you have any idea where Al might have gone?"

His frown was thoughtful. "Well, he used to work at the pawn shop some when we were short of roofing jobs. But I doubt he'd go there if he's hiding from the police."

Connor's radar ratcheted sky high. "What pawn shop?"

"They've got one down in Branson somewhere."

He glanced at his watch. "I need to call a taxi and get out of your way. Can you make it to Springfield to have Christmas with Carly and me?"

Steve accompanied him to the living room. "We have a job Monday, but we won't work Christmas Eve or Christmas Day. I'll leave right after work Monday and see you sometime that night."

As his dad drove him to the airport, Connor had two thoughts uppermost in his mind. They would be together as a family for Christmas.

And Lanell needed to know about that pawn shop.

Chapter 12

Lanell was getting ready to go to bed Saturday night when her phone rang. Seeing Connor's ID set a pogo stick amok in her chest.

"I've seen my dad," he said without preamble.

She wasn't sure what that could mean, or how to respond. "Is he doing okay?"

"He's fine, but he mentioned something that I thought you might find interesting. He said the reason he wanted to quit the All Star Roofing job—other than making better money—was because he had bad feelings about the people running it. A detail that came out in the conversation was the fact that the owners have a pawn shop in Branson."

An explosion of possibilities erupted in Lanell's brain. A burglary ring and a pawn shop fit like a hand in a glove. "Did he provide the name of it?"

"He didn't know the name or location. Can you find it?"

"I *will* find it," she said, determination coursing through her.

When they disconnected, she pulled out the Branson phone book she kept in a drawer of her bedside table and turned to the yellow pages. She made a list of all the pawn shops she found listed in Branson. Then she booted her computer and went to Leads Online, a web site that law enforcement used to locate missing items and individuals who could be instrumental in solving crimes.

After an hour of searching for items reported stolen from the schools, and names of suspects, she had found two cameras listed at one of those Branson shops that matched the descriptions of the ones stolen in the most recent school burglary.

She called Connor back. “Sorry if I woke you.”

“I had gone to bed, but hadn’t fallen asleep yet,” he said, sounding sort of groggy.

“I found a connection between a couple of cameras and a pawn shop in Branson. Now that school is out for the holidays, I’m working regular patrol. I’m sure Evan and the captain will want me to follow up on this when I tell them about it Monday morning. Would you like to visit that pawn shop with me?”

“I have a safety meeting that morning, but nothing that can’t be handled by Justin or someone else in the afternoon.”

“How about I pick you up shortly after noon? We can grab a bite of lunch somewhere and eat it on the way.”

“That sounds good. Should I be at the airport or my apartment?”

“Your apartment,” she decided after a moment’s consideration. “What’s the address?”

He gave it to her, and they ended the call.

Lanell was considering whether to go to church the next morning, but the decision was made for her when she got called to fill in for an officer who had called in sick. Now that she was working, she wished she could go to that pawn shop today, knowing from its web site that it was open on Sundays during the summer and Christmas tourist seasons. It would be a good time to see inside it without raising alarms, but she had already arranged for Connor to accompany her tomorrow. So she would wait.

Monday morning was overcast, and it was beginning to sprinkle as she left the apartment. The forecast was for temperatures slightly above freezing by late afternoon, and possible freezing rain that evening. But a break in the weather was predicted by late tomorrow, with higher temperatures and less rain.

When she pulled up at Connor's apartment, he had apparently been looking for her, because he came right out and crawled into the passenger seat. He brushed moisture from his coat, glancing over at her jeans and heavy, everyday coat. "I wasn't expecting to see you out of uniform, but still driving a patrol car."

She grinned. "I wore street clothes so I can go in the place as a regular shopper and take my time browsing. I don't plan on them seeing what I'm driving."

Lanell drove to a Burger King, and they bought hamburgers to go. They had eaten them by the time they were beyond the city limits. Patches of fog drifted across the highway, making visibility poor, as she worked her way south. She turned the radio to an easy listening station, needing something to distract her from the man sitting next to her.

She now believed his dad was not involved in the theft ring. Leaving so suddenly had not looked good, but learning of his unease about the men with whom he had been working spoke volumes. And he may have supplied a bit of information that would prove helpful.

As for Connor, he was hard to read. At times she sensed a mutual attraction. At others, he seemed far more interested in her murder case than in her.

The fog had nearly disappeared by the time they reached the outskirts of the city known for its wholesome entertainment venues. She shook off her preoccupying thoughts and concentrated on finding the pawn shop. When they identified it, she drove on around the corner of the block and parked where they wouldn't be seen getting out of a police vehicle.

The brick building boasted a row of six big glass window panes across the front of it, a hodgepodge of items visible through them. Inside, they paused and did a visual scan of the place. Gun racks lined the wall to their right. Small cases of shelves and bins stocked with every kind of small items were positioned in rows across the center of the huge, open building. It looked like larger items occupied the rear section.

"Is there something special you need?" the middle aged clerk asked from behind the L shaped counter near the front of the store asked.

"We're just browsing," she said, heading toward the guns.

She and Connor each selected a gun and examined it. Then they meandered about the room, looking over the goods. When she spotted some cameras, she zoomed in on them.

Sensing her intent, Connor positioned himself between her and the clerk to shield her while she took the list of serial numbers from her pocket and compared them to the half dozen cameras on the rack.

"Got it," she whispered in satisfaction when she found one listed on the web site. She rearranged the others back on the shelf, but held onto that one.

They started toward the back of the room, but she paused when she spotted a pitching machine in the corner. She made a beeline for it.

Connor reached it at the same time and began to inspect it. He ran a hand over the parts one by one, and moved to the tire. Then he bent over and peered closely at the wheel inside it. "I remember Dale talking about this one day."

"What?" Lanell looked at where he pointed. The

wheel had some dents in it.

He stood upright, a grin spreading across his face. "I'm getting a warm, fuzzy feeling. I remember Dale telling about having to replace the tire on their pitching machine. Her student aide removed it, but when she had trouble getting it back in place, she picked up a bat and pounded on it. As soon as Dale realized what was happening, she took the bat from the girl, but the damage was done. Thankfully, it was cosmetic rather than functional. The aide switched classes at the end of the semester," he added wryly.

"Mmm," Lanell murmured, her eyes narrowing in thought. "Does Dale have any special way of identifying departmental equipment? I don't have serial numbers for sports items."

He gazed upward, as if searching his memory. After several moments, he gave a nod and said, "I remember her saying at one time that she puts her initials somewhere inside the more expensive items."

They both eyed the machine that reminded Lanell of an alien space creature. Then they began examining it in closer detail.

"Hey, what are you doing?" the clerk barked, hurrying across the room toward them.

In spite of the unfriendly interruption, a jolt of exultation shot through Lanell when Connor grunted from his twisted neck position on the floor. "The letters DW are on the back of the control panel." He scrambled to his feet and faced the man. "We've just identified this piece of equipment as a machine that was stolen from a high school in Springfield."

The man's face blanched. He stopped and swallowed. "You're sure?"

Lanell pulled her badge from her purse and shoved it in front of him. Then she held up the camera. "This camera's serial number is on the list of photography equipment stolen more recently from another school. I'm going to call the detective in charge of the case and tell him about these items."

The man's eyes dilated, his gaze darting around the store, as if searching for help.

She proceeded to dial Evan. After a brief conversation, she extended the phone to the clerk. "The detective will identify himself and tell you to turn these things over to us."

The man's Adam's apple bobbed as he put the phone to his ear and listened. He responded with a "Yes, Sir" at intervals. When he returned the phone to her, he turned and preceded them to the front counter. "You have to sign for 'em," he said in a flat tone, pushing a form toward them.

Lanell wrote a brief note stating they were taking the items and why. She signed it and handed Connor the pen. "You're not an officer, but you're a witness."

He scrawled his name below hers.

"Thank you," she said to the clerk. "The detective will be here soon to talk to you. And we'll be outside watching until he gets here, so don't think of leaving."

On the way back to Springfield, Lanell wrestled her thoughts and emotions while keeping her eyes on the highway. It occurred to her that she and Connor had a good deal in common, each having lost their parents at a young age. The difference was that he had now regained his dad—however damaged. He was bound to be concerned about the man's well-being.

"Will you get to see your dad for the holiday?" she asked, darting a glance over at him. At some point she had come to like him—as more than a friend—and care about his family relationships.

"He had to work today, but he said he's driving back here tonight to be with me and Carly for the holiday."

"Do you have big plans for tomorrow or Christmas Day?"

He shifted in the seat and gave her a long searching look. "I have to make a short run in the morning, but I'll be home before noon. Carly has to work the second shift. So I figured I'd take her and Dad out to a nice restaurant between my getting home and Carly leaving."

An uncharacteristic impulse struck Lanell. "Why don't you come to my place? I'll pick up some things at the grocery store tonight, and make a nice meal for all of us."

"You don't have other plans?"

Reading surprise in his face, she shrugged and directed her gaze straight ahead. "I had thought I might splurge and have a milkshake with my tuna sandwich."

The interior of the car seemed to shrink and close in around them. It felt warmer.

"You actually want company, don't you?" he asked in what sounded like wonder.

She glanced over, nodded jerkily, and returned her focus to the highway.

"We'll plan on it then. I'll let you know if either Carly or Dad can't make it."

Warm pleasure crept through her. She tamped down on it to concentrate on business. "If you have time right now, we'll deliver these items to the police station, and then go talk to Dale while Evan goes to interview that pawn shop clerk."

"I've got time."

~

"The motive was clearly robbery," Dale asserted, her gaze focusing on Lanell, and then Connor as they sat around her dining table reviewing what they knew about the case. Justin had taken the afternoon off and was in the basement with the children.

Connor nodded, his heart aching for her. Between losing Vernon and dealing with the sudden appearance of the mother who had abandoned her and Derek as young teens, Dale had to be running on empty. "I agree. Vernon's arrival took them off guard, they panicked, and one of them grabbed a hammer—the first thing handy—and killed him. What do you think?" he asked Lanell.

Her smoky blue eyes fixed on him. "I think there were at least two thieves, but there could have been more to carry stuff out of that shop. Some of it had to be heavy and cumbersome. They had a truck to haul it, and tire prints indicate there was a smaller vehicle, possibly a pickup, parked not far from the big truck. There may have been one person in each truck, but could have been two. My instinct says only one each. Evan surmises that they got busy and didn't hear Vernon's truck until he was right outside the building."

"They broke a window," he said, to keep the brainstorming flowing.

Lanell nodded. "The fragments of broken glass indicate it was broken from the inside, so they entered through the door. The lock isn't damaged, which means they had a key. And that brings us to the question of who had access to keys."

Dale regarded them steadily. "Staff members have keys. Support staff employees have keys. Maintenance workers have keys. For all I know, the students have keys. Family and friends of staff could get hold of keys and make copies. I have keys," she finished, her expression troubled, her hand motions agitated.

Connor wanted to reassure her, but didn't know how. He looked at Lanell. "My dad could have snitched a key from her and made a copy, but he didn't."

"No, he didn't," she affirmed. "He's no longer a suspect."

But he had been. Connor squelched the hurt and

focused on finding who had done it.

"We're doing that," she said quickly. "Evan has been interviewing staff and clearing them as quickly as he's able."

"Are any of them implicating colleagues?" Dale wanted to know, her thought processes understandable.

"Evan has never indicated such a thing," Lanell said, reaching for her coffee.

"What about administrators?" Connor asked. "Are they being considered and interviewed?"

Lanell eyed him over the rim of the mug, sipped, and put it down. "Of course they are." She turned toward Dale. "Let's organize our thoughts a little better, establish a chain of events. You can bet Evan's done that, but it might cause us to think of something new, however small, that could prove helpful."

Connor watched Dale's expression lighten a bit. "It's worth a try. It started when you two found the body."

He sipped at his coffee, waiting for one of them to continue. When he saw Dale's face whiten, he regretted his bluntness.

"After the robbery," Lanell said swiftly, "there were prowlers around the administration building who turned out to be young boys looking for cap pistols that had been confiscated. The administration and the boys' parents have dealt with them, but Connor and I went back to that area later and met some other boys who gave us a description of a truck that led us to All Star Roofing."

"My dad worked for that company," he tossed in crisply.

"He's no longer a suspect," she repeated briefly and went on. "Evan has been interviewing not only staff, but anyone else who raises suspicions."

"Carly's friend Donna left her abusive husband,

who's a petty thief and has since been arrested. Could he have graduated to bigger things and also be hooked up with this ring?"

Lanell's expression turned thoughtful. "I don't think so, but I'll have Evan find out more about him." She took a notepad from her purse and jotted a note.

"Then there was that last school robbery," Dale said.

Lanell's eyed darkened at the reminder. "The guy who was shot and died was known as Tark. His real name was Marlin Tarkington. Before he died, he said Al got away. We assume he meant his partner. He didn't seem to be concerned about anyone else, which is why we think there were only the two of them."

Dale drew a sharp breath, obviously steeling herself. "Alvin, I understand, turned out to be a brother to one of our school janitors, the one who just happens to be living with my mother. I can't tell you how much that worries me."

Lanell frowned. "We have to consider Claude. Evan interviewed him. He claims he was at home with your mother the night of the robbery, and he hasn't seen his brother in weeks. Your mother corroborated that he was with her during that time, and says she's never met the brother."

"Claude has keys that he could have copied and given to someone," Connor pointed out, hating it for Dale's sake, but forced to be honest.

~

Lanell glanced at Dale as Connor spoke haltingly and decided to move on to another subject. "I think the items we recovered from that pawn shop establish a link between the last robbery and the one at our school. They had an item from each school. It must be the same thieves."

Connor emitted a soft chuckle. “That clerk looked like he had swallowed a horse when you shoved your badge at him.”

She couldn’t prevent a grin at the memory. “He’s probably fully aware that hot merchandise is being moved through there. I’m anxious to find out how Evan’s talk with him went.”

“The owners of the All Star Roofing Company and that pawn shop have to be behind the whole operation,” Dale said, her fists clenched in anger, her coffee forgotten.

“Both Hamilton brothers have alibis for each robbery time frame,” Lanell pointed out.

“So they’re sending their stooges to do their dirty work,” Dale retorted hotly.

“You’re probably right. But we have to prove it, and find out which stooge did the killing.”

Sounds indicated that Justin and the youngsters were coming up the stairs.

On one hand, the past hour or so of tossing around ideas and theories didn’t seem to have gotten them any closer to catching Vernon’s killer. On the other hand, Lanell’s brain was stirring in a way she couldn’t quite bring into focus. She felt that she might have missed something at the murder scene.

She and Connor put on their coats and went to her cruiser. The drive back to his apartment was quiet, each lost in private thoughts.

“Will you come inside for a while?” he asked when she pulled to a stop outside his apartment and let the motor idle. “We can have snacks, or watch TV, or …something.”

She met his look. “It sounds nice, but I have to report back to the department and meet with Evan.”

“I’m not ready to go inside yet,” he said quietly, an odd quality to his voice that sent a shiver over her nerve endings.

The pupils of his eyes darkened, and he slid over closer to her. The air shifted as his gaze traveled over her features in such intense scrutiny that her lips tingled. She felt herself flushing.

He reached over, sliding even closer, and gently cupped her cheek with a palm. Their gazes collided, taking stock, wondering.

Her heart thudded at the realization that he was going to kiss her. And there was nothing impetuous about it this time. Disjointed thoughts raced around and collided madly in her mind. She was crazy to want this.

When his fingertips traced along the edge of her jaw and tucked a strand of hair behind her ear, she didn't pull away. Then, when he bent his head and kissed her with exquisite tenderness, her heart turned over with sweet joy. It felt so right.

The world around them faded away, and Lanell didn't know how long they were locked in the embrace. When he drew back, she slowly returned to the real world, questioning what had just happened.

He cupped her cheek again and sighed. "I'm not sorry I did that, and I hope you're not either. I have a lot to think about. I'm feeling things I've never felt before."

She smiled. "I have some serious thinking to do as well."

It took all her will power to watch him slide out of the car and walk away.

Chapter 13

Connor was glad when he had his charter group delivered to their Christmas party in Hawaii the next morning. He would return for them Friday.

He settled back into the cockpit and prepared to head home. The engines roared, and the plane began to taxi forward. Then it built speed until the nose tipped skyward, and he experienced the thrill of flight that never grew old. Seconds later the back wheels lifted, and he was airborne—headed home to his family—and Lanell.

When he landed at the Springfield airport, he wasted no time getting to his vehicle and heading to his apartment to meet Steve and Carly. Carly had surprised him at her willingness to have dinner with Lanell. Steve had required a bit of persuasion, but not too much. After his dad's arrival last night, they had gone to the mall and done some shopping. Their loot was still stashed in the rear of his SUV.

Suddenly he wondered if there would be an opportunity to repeat yesterday's kiss. Just the memory of it made his heart beat faster. He tucked the thought inside his chest.

He wasn't sure it was a good idea to be in love with Lanell, but he was sure by now that he had no control over the matter. He was head over heels. But did she feel the same way?

By the time they arrived at Lanell's apartment in a middle class subdivision, he had a knot the size of a bowling ball in his stomach. Beside him, Steve's head rotated slightly as he scanned the neighborhood. "Looks nice," he commented.

The door opened before anyone could ring the bell. Smiling, Lanell stuck a hand out toward Steve, her dark blue eyes friendly, and assessing. It appeared that any suspicions or negative feelings she had toward Steve were truly gone. "Come in," she greeted them, swinging the door back further.

Connor's impression of the apartment was homey. The furniture looked like it had been around a while, but the green and gray color blend worked for him. Knowing that she didn't look forward to Christmas, he wasn't surprised to see no tree or decorations about the apartment.

The smell of home cooked food emanating from the kitchen made his stomach react. Lanell looked natural here, wearing comfortable gray slacks and a red sweatshirt and holding a dishtowel in one hand, a direct contrast to her work persona.

"Come on to the table and have a seat," she said, leading the way into her small kitchen. The meal that was spread before them at a small table that had been enlarged with two center extensions consisted of a big platter of turkey, dressing, and sweet potatoes, as well as mashed potatoes and gravy. As they settled, she positioned bowls of salad at each place setting. They bowed their heads while Connor said a blessing.

"Mmm, this is delicious," Steve said a few minutes later, after downing a big helping of turkey. "You've outdone yourself, Miss Rhodes."

"Call me Lanell," she insisted.

He nodded. "You're a good cook, Lanell."

She smiled. "Thanks. I enjoy cooking—if I don't

have to do it too often."

Connor thought he detected a wistful note in her tone. Did she yearn to cook for someone besides just herself—a family?

This was nice. It felt good. Too good.

"There's plenty," she said. "I'll probably be eating leftovers for a week. And I made chocolate pies."

"Now, don't start drooling, Son," Steve said, chuckling.

Connor gave Lanell a sheepish look. "I'm a choco-o-holic."

"Me, too," echoed around the table.

Connor cleared his throat and spoke to Lanell. "Dale always expects us at her house Christmas afternoon for snacks and board games. She considers us extended family. And she wants to include you this year."

Jaw dropping surprise registered on her face. "I …uh, I don't know what to say."

"Don't say anything. Just come. Meet us there at two o'clock," Carly said, making it a sassy directive.

All this was causing images to float through Connor's mind. The thought of eating together like this regularly. Lanell and Steve being part of Dale's extended family. A funny lump formed in his chest.

Even though he knew he shouldn't build dream castles in the air.

~

After her company had left, Lanell was restless. She paced the floor, her thoughts jumping from one thing to another. She yanked her shirt sleeves down, having pushed them nearly to her elbows while working in the kitchen, and stared morosely out the window at the lightly falling snow.

Connor Prescott appealed to her in a way no one

ever had, unnerving her. He was honorable and strong, yet soft on the inside. He had suffered loss and hurt in his youth, yet found strength and solace in God—unlike her rejection.

Remorse stabbed at her. Had she only made her life harder? Yes, she probably had, by isolating herself, trying to be self-sufficient. She had been alone for years—and empty.

Her gaze rose heavenward, wondering if God could really make a difference. Searching her heart, she knew she needed more than she had. Her eyes squeezed shut.

"Help me, Lord. Let me know if you really care. Make my life more meaningful. Give me more purpose."

As she stood there in supplication, a sense of peace washed over her. "Thank you, God," she whispered.

As she opened her eyes, an urge to share her new perspective came over her—and an unbidden image of Connor's face rose in her mind. And that brought recollections of the way he had kissed her.

It may not have been such a big deal to him, but it had rocked her world. Now she faced the reason. Sought or not, strong feelings for him had taken root, developed—and grown into love. She tucked the knowledge into the recesses of her heart.

As she did, a renewed sense of purpose filled her. She shook off her lethargy and donned her professional persona. She went to the computer, determined to turn up some new information that would help catch a killer.

Anticipating success where failure had so far resulted, she began another data search on Claude and Leona. She located several articles and read until her eyes grew tired, but learned nothing new. She was convinced that Claude was connected to the burglaries. He hadn't killed Vernon, but he likely knew who had. She still harbored the feeling that he was urging Leona to take advantage of her daughter, find ways to squeeze money out of her. He looked and acted so harmless, but Lanell's instincts said he wasn't. Mere hunches weren't enough. She needed to find solid evidence that would prove it.

Disappointed when she had read until her eyes burned and still found nothing helpful, she leaned back in the chair, rubbing them, and tried to think what to do next.

After chasing several elusive ideas to nowhere, she went to her personal folder that included files Evan had shared with her regarding this case, and let her gaze drift over the file names. One of them made her pause. It was the list of drugs stolen from that pharmacy near the school back during the time the rash of school burglaries had begun. Lanell opened the file and scanned it, fragmented facts and thoughts flying hither and yon in her brain.

Something nagged at her, but she couldn't make the connection. She stopped reading and called Evan. Yes, it was Christmas Eve. But murder cases paid no attention to holidays or their meaning.

"Yeah," he greeted her, sounds of a TV blaring beyond him. "I thought you would be kicking back, taking it easy by now." Since her work schedule coincided with the school's, she didn't have to work the holidays when classes were dismissed.

"That doesn't mean my brain shuts down," she retorted. "What can you tell me about Donna Echols' husband, other than that she filed a report about him abusing her, and she was able to escape to the women's shelter?"

"That about covers it. What line of reasoning are you chasing?"

"I know Jack's a thief. I'm wondering if he's also a drug user or dealer."

"Give me a minute."

Lanell shifted the phone to her other ear, and then back again minutes later. She knew Evan was a computer genius and could access more police sites from home than she could, but waiting was still hard. Then he was back.

"I found no drug related arrests. His game is stealing. What are you thinking?"

"I was wondering if he's connected to those school burglaries. But then I looked at that last drug theft. It's different, a break from an established pattern."

"I agree," he said. "The ring has been stealing items from schools that they know they can pawn. It doesn't seem that they're into drug dealing. Yet these drug thefts are happening in the same parts of town as the school burglaries, at near the same time."

"So, is it the same bunch, or do we have another thief, or thieves?"

"I'm not sure," he admitted. "This case sure is disrupting Christmas."

Lanell thanked him for his help and ended the call. But she couldn't end the parade of questions marching through her mind. She stared at the drug list that was still on the computer screen. Then she located the list of drugs taken in the pharmacy robberies. Slowly it filtered through her brain that the drugs Dale's mother said she needed were on each list. She had said she had prescriptions at Walgreens, yet none had been filled at those pharmacies. Was it possible that Claude had stolen those lots of drugs to get the ones Leona needed without it being evident exactly which ones he was after—and she could have her prescription drugs without paying for them, and pocket the money obtained from her daughter?

While that idea percolated, she pulled up the crime scene photos, thinking another look couldn't hurt. She examined them closely, one by one. Then she paused at one and leaned closer. Not sure what she was seeing, she opened that one in a photo enhancing software program and enlarged it on the screen.

Her heart began to pound, a picture forming in her mind.

She called Evan back.

"What now?" His tone was somewhere between interest and impatience.

She explained what she had noticed, and what she thought it meant.

"Are you ready to help me flush these guys out?" he asked after going over everything in detail.

"Just tell me what to do," she shot back.

After devising a plan for tomorrow and ending the call, Lanell remembered Connor and Carly's invitation to the Whitaker home for the afternoon. Already unsure of Connor's feelings for her, and uncomfortable about intruding on Dale's personal life so much, she decided God must be telling her that her job was priority.

Once again she picked up her phone. She texted Connor.

Something has come up. Can't make it tomorrow.

~

Christmas morning Connor crawled out of bed and found Steve at the kitchen stove. He looked over and paused in stirring something in a skillet. "You want an omelet?"

"Sure, since you're cooking. Do I need to make toast?"

"Not for me."

When they finished eating, Connor eyed the omelet still on the platter. "You think Carly will eat that?"

Steve shrugged. "I doubt it, even though I made it for her. She's never been a heavy breakfast eater. By the time she gets done sleeping in, a bowl of cereal is probably the most she'll want." He grinned. "You thinking someone else might be hungry?"

Connor returned the grin. "I'll take it to her, and be back here shortly. Maybe Carly will be up by then, and we'll have our gift exchange."

Steve nodded. "Sounds like a plan."

Minutes later Connor rang Lanell's doorbell.

Her eyes widened in surprise when she opened the door. "Are you checking up on me?" The question didn't sound negative—but almost as if she liked the idea.

"I just wanted to say Merry Christmas. Here's a sample of Dad's cooking." He handed her the foil wrapped omelet. "You'll have to zap it."

She hesitated a moment, but then took it and stepped back. "Come in."

He did, but didn't take a seat. He studied her expression. "You look pretty chipper this morning."

She smiled. "I'm less tense than I have been."

He tilted his head. "Is there a special reason?"

"I discovered you're right about God—that I was wrong to blame Him for all that went wrong in my life, and that I need Him. I've asked His forgiveness and found peace."

His heart nearly burst. He was thrilled for her—whether or not her new outlook on life included him. He wanted to pull her into his arms, but sensed she wasn't ready for that. "Do you know yet who killed Vernon?"

Her expression went solemn. "I think so, but we have to prove it."

"By we, do you mean you and the detective?"

"Yes."

"That's what came up, isn't it?"

She nodded without speaking.

He tried to read her mind, but of course couldn't. "You're planning something. It'll be dangerous, won't it?"

She shrugged. "There's always that possibility. But

we're careful."

"And you're not going to tell me your plan."

"I can't. It's police business—and I can't involve a civilian."

His heart thunked. "Your job means everything to you, doesn't it?"

Her expression went resolute, and he thought he read regret in her eyes. But deep inside him, he faced the fact that he had been right. Her job came first and last. She no longer needed him.

He drew a long breath of painful acceptance and opened the door. "I hope your plan, whatever it is, is successful."

He turned and hustled to his vehicle, needing to escape before she read the defeat in his face.

Chapter 14

Lanell removed yesterday's leftover pie from the refrigerator and placed it in a plastic carrier. A knot of tension curled in her stomach. She paused and took a deep breath, willing her nerves to relax. When she felt steady, she put on her coat and left the apartment.

It was two o'clock in the afternoon. A fine mist of rain was falling from the sky and adding to the wet slush on the side streets. She knew the main highways were clear, although wet, but the already near freezing temperature was still dropping.

She drove her sedan to Aurora and located the address Evan had given her. It was a small frame house no longer very white, with dark green shutters. It sat on a corner lot, where the ditches surrounding it were filled with uncut, brown grass and weeds. The older model pickup she recognized as having seen Claude drive to work was parked at the side of the back yard.

When Lanell knocked at the door, she didn't hear anything for several moments. Then footsteps came slowly toward the door. It squeaked open, and Leona's square-like face peered through the narrow opening. Lanell couldn't help but notice that she wasn't using her cane.

The sour look on the woman's face was quickly replaced by an expression of dawning recognition. "Well, hello, Miss School Cop. I almost didn't recognize you in regular clothes instead of your uniform. Sorry I can't remember your name. What can I do for you?"

Lanell held the pie toward her. "I had this left from a big meal yesterday and wondered if you and Claude might like it. It's chocolate."

Dark eyes lit. "It sounds delicious."

"May I come inside and remove it from the carrier? I'd like to take it back home with me."

"Of course." The woman stepped back and opened the door wider.

As she led the way, Lanell followed her into the kitchen. Claude sat at the table, nursing a cup of coffee. He looked up, and surprise registered on his face. "Well, look who's here," he said, getting to his feet.

"She's brought us a pie," Leona said. "Isn't that nice?"

Lanell placed it on the table and removed the cover. "It's meant for eating."

She glanced around as Leona opened a cabinet and drawer and drew out a knife. The place wasn't very tidy. Maybe cleaning only happened when there was a paycheck attached.

"Would you like a cup of coffee?" Claude asked.

"That sounds good." It provided the excuse she needed to linger a bit and strike up a conversation. She kept her coat on so she could leave quickly.

"Did you bake this yourself?" Leona asked, sliding a saucer with a generous slice on it in front of Claude.

Lanell smiled. "I did. I live alone and don't cook a lot. But occasionally I invite friends in and cook a big meal, so I don't forget how," she added in a light tone.

"I don't cook much either," Leona said. "I can't be on my feet very long at a time."

Lanell still hadn't spotted the woman's cane. She didn't seem to need it much.

"Who did you cook for yesterday?" Claude asked,

his brow doing a little suggestive arch. “Was it a young man?”

She made a noncommittal half grimace and shrugged. “Maybe.”

He chuckled. Then he turned serious. “Have the police figured out who killed Vernon?”

Lanell hesitated, letting him think she was debating how much she could say. “I’m not at liberty to reveal details, but they know the brothers who own All Star Roofing are behind the ring burglarizing the schools. And we know the name of the partner of the man who was shot in that last robbery,” she added in a tone of confidentiality. “Just before he died, Tark told us.”

Watching the startled reaction in Claude’s eyes, she continued. “The funny thing is, the man who’s on the run has the same last name as you. His name is Jenkins. Al Jenkins.”

“It’s not Jenks,” erupted from his mouth.

The abbreviated name whizzed through Lanell’s brain. Now she was no longer guessing. She knew for sure. Tark had not told her he was jinxed. He had named Vernon’s killer—Jenks. It took every bit of self-control she had to not fire back that she knew otherwise.

She managed to keep her face impassive, hoping Claude would continue to believe that, as an employee of the school, he was an insider and was being trusted with confidential information. “Our detective got an anonymous tip from someone saying he thinks he knows where this Al is hiding. I think they plan to arrest him this afternoon.”

She saw Leona stifle a gasp. Claude’s face had gone rigid. But he forked a bite of pie into his mouth. “Mm, this is good,” he mumbled.

Lanell took a swig of coffee and set the cup down. “Glad you like it. I need to be going.” She stood and picked up the pie carrier.

Both of them thanked her again, and Leona accompanied her to the door.

Lanell got in her car and pulled into the street. Then she drove around the block and parked next to the ditch beside a vacant lot, close enough to observe the house she had just left without being seen by the occupants.

Within minutes Claude emerged, with Leona clinging to his belt behind his back, and arguing, apparently expressing her intent of going with him. When she refused to let go, he grabbed her hand and practically dragged her across the yard and around to the passenger door of the old pickup. He had to push her up into the seat. Then he hurried around to the driver's side, climbed behind the wheel, and started the motor.

Lanell spoke into her shoulder receiver. "They took the bait. They're on the move."

"We're in position," Evan responded.

She waited until the pickup headed down the street and rounded the corner. Then she started her car and followed, keeping far enough back to not be noticed.

As Claude drove out of town and traffic grew heavier, Lanell gave Evan a location update. "It looked like he was heading back into Springfield, but he just veered off onto Highway 60."

As Lanell turned to follow the pickup off the main highway, her tires lost traction and started sliding. She slowed down and regained control, staring straight ahead and praying she didn't lose sight of her quarry. The roads were getting slick.

The pickup slowed as it approached a trailer park, and then turned. Lanell estimated twenty to thirty trailers behind the tall wooden fence.

When Claude steered to a stop beside one of the trailers near the end of a row, she pulled to the side of the street and parked to watch what they did.

Claude got out of the truck and turned in the

doorway, speaking across the seat to Leona. It appeared he was ordering her to stay in the truck. He slammed the door shut and chugged to the door of the trailer. Moments later he disappeared inside.

Lanell waited about a minute and then dialed Claude's cell phone number she had gotten from his school employee records. "Yeah," he growled.

"You need to tell Al to come outside and give himself up. It'll make things easier on him."

"You double crossing sneak," he bellowed, recognizing her voice. The line went dead.

Lanell started the car and drove up to that trailer. As she turned into the driveway, she detected motion to the right rear of the trailer. A man, she assumed Al, crawled into the cab of a dark colored truck with a flatbed behind it. The motor started, and it peeled out. At the same time, Claude raced to his pickup and did likewise.

"They're running," she informed Evan, backing out of the drive.

"We have two cars just down the street from the park entrance. You keep behind us."

Since she was driving her personal vehicle, she had no siren or police lights. As she drove toward the exit, the fleeing vehicles careened out of the trailer park and headed south.

Up ahead, two police cars sped after them, sirens screaming. Already falling behind, Lanell shoved the gas pedal to the floorboard, but continued to fall even further behind them.

A couple of minutes later, an overhead light came into view up ahead. It was green. But it turned red as Al's speeding vehicle reached it and went flying on through it. Claude's brake lights flashed. At the same time, a semi coming toward them braked, and went into a screeching skid on the ice glazed pavement.

The semi plowed into Claude's pickup, and the

crash of metal on metal set Lanell's heart pounding. The pickup flipped over and slid to a halt at the side of the highway, while the semi tumbled down into the ditch. Lanell tapped her brakes carefully to slow down without going into a similar slide.

One police car pulled to the verge, while the other swerved past the havoc and continued its pursuit of Al. Evan's voice filled her ear. "Josh is going after the killer. You and I will work this mess. Call 9 1 1."

Lanell made the call and drove up behind Evan's parked patrol car. She climbed out and ran to catch up to him, shivering from the cold and pulling the hoodie of her coat over her head for protection from the icy mist.

Evan headed at a run for the semi. "You check the pickup," he yelled over his shoulder.

She ran to it, slipping and sliding on the wet surface, and yanked open the door. What she saw sent her heart plummeting.

~

Connor traced invisible circles on the table top with an index finger, his mind drifting far from Justin and Dale's dining room and the board game they were playing. The scents of lasagna and garlic bread lingered from the big meal they had eaten earlier.

"It's your turn, Bro."

Carly's voice snapped him to attention. But he couldn't for the life of him remember what play he had meant to execute—or if he even had one in mind.

While trying to regain some sense of the game, his cell phone rang. When he looked at the ID, he blinked. Had Lanell known he was thinking of her?

"Hello," he said guardedly.

"Are you at home?" she asked in a voice that struck him as strained.

"No, I'm at the Whitakers." She should have known

that, since she had been invited, and then cancelled.

An audible breath sounded across the line. "There's been a wreck. It's serious. Dale's mother and her companion were involved. Can you get Dale to the hospital quickly? I'm following the ambulance. We should be there in about five minutes."

"Which one?" He held his breath as she told him to meet her at Cox Medical. "We'll be there as fast as possible."

When he disconnected, he looked across the table at Dale's apprehensive expression. "Your mother and Claude have been in an accident. The ambulance is on the way to Cox."

"Don't worry about those two." Carly nodded at the two youngsters sitting on the carpet, playing with their toys. "I'll look after them."

Justin hurried to get their coats. "You can call Derek as soon as we're in the car," he said to his wife as he held her coat for Dale to slip her arms into it.

Ashen faced, she only nodded.

"We can all go in my vehicle," Connor offered.

Justin considered for only a moment. "No, we should each take our own. There's no telling when we might …need it."

Connor agreed. He aimed a look at Carly and mouthed a thank-you at her as he shoved his arms into his own coat. "We'll update you," he promised softly.

When he walked into the hospital minutes later, he spied Lanell leaning against the wall near the information desk, her expression solemn. She simultaneously saw him, straightened, and started toward him.

"Is this the something that came up?" he asked as they met halfway.

She nodded in short, jerky motions. "Vernon's killer has been arrested. Claude's truck collided with a semi. It's bad. I'll give you the details later," she said as Justin and Dale appeared inside the entrance. "They're going to need your support."

He nodded and followed her back to meet them. Dale hurried directly to Lanell. "What happened? Where are they?"

Lanell placed her hands on Dale's arm. "They're with the doctors. We have to wait for word. We can go back to the emergency room waiting area if you'd like."

When Dale nodded, Lanell guided her back to her husband and led them down the hall. At the waiting area, Justin steered Dale to a pair of seats and pulled her down beside him.

The sight of their worried faces and Dale's quivering chin tore at Connor. He looked at Lanell. Seeing that she shared his emotions, he wanted to pull her to a seat beside him as Justin had done with Dale. But he remembered that she was on duty and knew she wouldn't welcome any distractions—or him.

A few minutes later Derek arrived and joined their solemn vigil. He had barely gotten seated next to Dale and heard some explanations when a doctor stepped through the doorway.

He tugged the surgical cap from his head and did a visual sweep of the room. When Dale and Derek rose to their feet, he approached them. "Are you the family of Mr. Jenkins or Mrs. Denning?"

"Mrs. Denning is our mother," Derek said.

"Will you come with me? You may bring your family." His gaze moved to Lanell. "Are you with them?"

She nodded. "I'm a friend, but also the police officer who was present at the accident."

The doctor nodded approval and led them into a small room across the hall. Connor took it as a bad sign and steeled himself.

"I'm sorry," the doctor said gently. "Neither of them made it."

While one part of his brain absorbed that sad fact, Connor suddenly realized that it was time for Carly to go to work and that she would need to find someone to relieve her from babysitting duties. The Whitakers couldn't deal with any more right now. Seeing no other option, he backed away and slipped silently through the doorway.

~

Lanell watched the twin siblings absorb the information in passive silence, their faces frozen. She wanted them to cry—or something—but they didn't.

"Thank you, doctor," Derek finally said. "Please have your staff call the Farrell Funeral Home for our mother." He glanced at Dale, and she nodded agreement.

Lanell spoke up. "Mr. Jenkins' brother has been arrested. I'll see that he's informed about Claude so he can make arrangements."

The doctor thanked her and took his leave.

Lanell stepped over to Dale, needing to communicate with her, but unable to form words. Dale had become such a dear friend. Lanell's mouth trembled when she tried to speak.

Dale moved, and then they were hugging—and crying—together. After several moments, Lanell blubbered, "I lost my mother on Christmas Day."

Dale gripped her hands and locked gazes with her. "I lost mine long ago."

"She's right," Derek said quietly.

Lanell looked over the group, one by one, and realized that Connor had disappeared.

The only satisfaction she could derive from this Christmas Day was that they had gotten justice for Vernon.

Chapter 15

Connor ignored sounds of the dozen chattering passengers he had picked up in Jamaica and was flying home from their Christmas vacation. A sense of emptiness ate at him.

Steve had gone back to Colorado, and he and Carly worked such different hours that he didn't see much of her. So they had decided to remain roommates, at least a little longer.

Sadness came over him as Dale and Derek's situation continued to occupy his mind. He admired them for the way they were coping while hurting. They had decided to ship their mother back to Hot Springs, where they had grown up, for burial near her parents. They would have a small private service there tomorrow, conducted by the now retired minister who had been their childhood pastor.

Thoughts of Lanell gradually replaced those reflections, in spite of his efforts to prevent that from happening. As always, they brought a sense of giddiness—and longing. She had been wonderful to Dale and Justin, available for everything from child care to helping with funeral arrangements.

She was good at her job, and seemed to love it. Did she consider it enough to fill her entire life, or would she consider sharing it with someone? Him.

He loved her. And he thought—hoped—she loved

him. But he was afraid to find out. He longed for a family, one founded on faith in God. But did she want the same thing?

His mind flashed back to the business at hand. He landed at the airport and watched his passengers exit the plane, still chattering with animation about their stay on the island.

Back in his office, his mind drifted, unable to stay focused on airline matters.

An hour after quitting time, Justin stepped into the office. He wore a near scowl. "What are you still doing here?"

Connor tried to work his brain around his boss's expression—and couldn't. He opted for defense. "You're still here, aren't you?"

Justin's mouth curved around in a half amused way. "I've been getting things in order to leave in the morning. What's your excuse?"

"I guess I don't have one." In view of what his boss and Dale were dealing with, he didn't.

Justin dragged a chair over near the desk and plopped down in it. "You're hiding."

Connor's jaw tightened. "You're meddling."

Justin's brow arched. "I was guessing. But I'm right. Can you deny that you're in love, and hedging over what to do about it?"

He couldn't, so he didn't try.

Justin leaned back in the chair, arms folded across his chest. "You have a lot in common with both Lanell and my wife, the loss of your parents and learning to take care of yourselves at an early age. But you and Dale had something Lanell didn't."

Connor let that buzz through his brain. "You mean Carly, don't you?"

His boss nodded. "You had her. Dale had Derek. You both had companionship."

"Lanell had no one," Connor murmured. "And she didn't have the kind of Christian environment we had. I understand that. But it doesn't mean she loves me."

Justin's brow arched. "Dale and I have watched both of you. Trust me, that gal loves you."

The certainty in his tone gave Connor courage. And the knowledge that he had to convince Lanell they belonged together.

He stood. "I guess if I can fly planes, I can fly against the odds."

Justin grinned. "You heading to her place?"

"Not yet."

He was going shopping. Ring shopping.

~

"Hey, Rhodes, I need you on the streets today," the captain said as Lanell entered the police station Monday morning expecting to spend the day in the office. "We've got two guys using vacation time, another just called in sick, and we've already got a fender bender over on Chestnut. Get your tail over there."

She saluted and headed back out. She had to work a full shift today, but was supposed to get off early tomorrow and be off all the next day for New Year's. School would resume Thursday the second.

Once the minor accident had been dealt with and reports completed, the day continued in hectic fashion. She assumed people were mobbing the malls and shops to return or exchange Christmas gifts—or shopping for greatly reduced Christmas wrappings and such for next year.

By quitting time, she was more than ready to go home and fall asleep on the couch. She still liked her job, but it was no longer enough in itself. She was lonely. She looked forward to returning to school Thursday, yet dreaded it. Seeing friends and students would be good, but she was certain to face a barrage of questions about the robberies and deaths—especially that of their missing janitor. That would not be good.

Claude had been the inside man at her school, and had supplied the thieves with copies of keys—probably lifted from janitors who worked in other parts of the school, and Dale's key to the sports shed—and had provided information on locations of the most valuable items to take and where to find them. His captured brother had admitted as much.

Lanell had correctly envisioned all that when she spotted the mop bucket with the pink paint smudge on it in one of the crime photos. She theorized that Claude had pushed that thing around to have an excuse for being in areas not on his usual assigned work zones, and had gone to the shop during the shift he worked the Friday night before the Sunday night burglary. He had parked it in that corner of the room and gotten busy—possibly making a list of which items for his pals to take from there—and forgotten it.

She had also confirmed from fingerprints found at the pharmacy that had been robbed last that Claude had indeed been stealing drugs, taking a mixture that included the ones being prescribed for Leona.

Another success had been learning that the Hamilton brothers owned multiple pawn shops and moved hot items around amongst them. Employees who worked at the stores were aware that they were fencing hot items, and encouraged shoplifters to bring them valuable stuff. They would pay the shoplifters around ten cents on the dollar for them, stock some in the shops, and sell others on Amazon and eBay. Then they would mail them to locations all around the country. Raids on the shops had netted thousands of dollars' worth of stolen property.

Sentences were expected to range from years in

prison, to jail time, thousands in fines, and community service.

As she signed out and headed to her car, a sequence of scenes filtered through Lanell's mind—finding the body, the crash, the hospital scene, and the jolt she had felt when she realized Connor had disappeared. Later she learned that he had gone to relieve Carly from babysitting so she could go to work.

As she scooted behind the wheel, her cell phone rang. She was reluctant to answer it, until she saw Dale's I. D. "Hello."

"Will you join us at Connor's apartment tomorrow evening for a New Year's Eve dinner? He said since he ate Christmas meals at your place and ours, he figures it's his turn to balance the tables—whatever that means."

Lanell hesitated, wishing desperately to see Connor, but not in a crowd. She started to decline, but couldn't do that to Dale. "What time?"

"He said we should come at five, but the food may not be ready until closer to six. And, no, we're not to bring anything," she added, anticipating the next question.

Lanell's gut clenched the next evening as she drove up the street to the Prescott apartment. It was ten after five, so she was surprised to see no familiar vehicles parked in front of the building.

She swallowed a lump of nervousness as she rang the bell.

Connor swung the door open. "Hello, Lady Lanell," he said, his gaze taking in the fitted slacks and emerald green top she wore beneath her gray coat. She returned the appraisal, appreciating his casual look in jeans and a light blue shirt. He looked more handsome to her every time she saw him.

"Give me your coat," he said as she stepped inside.

She glanced around the living room, neither seeing

nor hearing anyone. A Christmas tree stood in lonely splendor, its lights twinkling.

"The Whitakers couldn't make it," he said before she could ask. "Carly had to work."

She certainly understood that. Cops worked twenty-four-seven, being needed during holidays as much as, or more than, any other time.

"Our steaks are ready." He took her hand and led her into a kitchen similar to her small one.

The meal was good, the steaks tender, the baked potatoes smothered in butter and sour cream, all preceded by nice salads. Dessert was a coconut cream pie. "Carly made it before she left," Connor confessed as he cut slices for each of them.

When they finished eating, he seemed to lose his air of confidence. After letting her help clean up the kitchen, he turned to face her and cleared his throat. He took her hand in his. "We've both had some Christmases in our youth that were less than memorable. I'd like to make up for that, start a tradition of happy ones, together. I know you didn't come expecting this." His head motion indicated where they had eaten, and then the tree visible through the living room doorway.

Like a puppet, Lanell let him lead her into the living room and tug her down onto the sofa beside him. Then he reached over and picked up the package that rested on the floor beneath the Christmas tree.

A flutter formed in the pit of her stomach. She stared into his intense face and let him place the package in her hands. "I have nothing for you," she said, hardly able to squeeze the airy protest from her lungs.

"Yes, you do. You'll understand when you open that."

Lanell looked down, threads of hope—fear—excitement—running through her. With trembling fingers she unwrapped the package and found a smaller black velvet box inside. She gasped, her hand going over her mouth, and looked up at him, too stunned to speak.

Connor slid off the sofa onto one knee facing her. "Look under it," he said, pointing to a folded piece of paper.

Lanell picked up the note and opened it. *All I want from you is a kiss—that means yes.*

She swallowed, drowning in the message flaring from his eyes.

"Will you marry me?" he asked between short, whispered breaths.

Finding his vulnerability endearing, she placed a trembling palm on his cheek. Emboldened by what she was seeing and hearing, she declared, "I love you, Connor."

He let out a huge whoosh of air. "I love you, too, Lanell. And I want nothing more than to be loved by you and spend my life with you."

He took her hands, and a quiver ran from his own into them. "So will you marry me?"

With tears springing into her eyes, she slid to her knees before him. "Yes," she said, reaching up and pulling him to her. "I will. I'll marry you. I'll have your babies. And I'll grow old with you."

Then they were locked in one another's arms, sharing a kiss of love and the promise of a home like neither of them had ever known.

It was a miracle. Never again would Christmas be a time of sadness. From now on it would be a time of joy and peace—with God at the head of it.

Epilogue

The church fellowship hall was decorated with blue and white streamers and wedding bells, the colors deemed appropriate for the marriage of a police officer and a pilot. They had decided to wed during spring break, spend their first weekend as a married couple in Branson, and take a longer honeymoon when school ended for the summer.

The wedding had been such a rush of preparations and breathlessness that Lanell still couldn't quite grasp that she was now married to the handsome man seated to her left at the head table at the reception.

Connor's dad had served as his best man, and sat at the other side of him. Carly had been Lanell's maid of honor and sat to her right. Dale and Justin had been groomsman and bridesmaid, and their little Jennifer the flower girl. Since Jax was way too young to serve as a ring bearer, they had simply left the safekeeping of the ring and production of it at the right moment to Steve.

"How soon can we get out of here?" Connor whispered into Lanell's ear, unabashedly anxious for them to be alone.

Lanell tapped a finger against his chin. "Patience, Mr. Groom," she teased. "We don't want to be rude."

He shifted in his chair, grinning roguishly. "Yes, we do."

"Behave," she chided, patting his shoulder. "Finish

your cake and coffee."

"Yes, Ma'am," he said meekly.

"Hey, you two," Carly piped up, leaning forward and aiming a stern look at her brother. "You can survive a few more minutes of all our company. Then the two of you have a lifetime to spend together."

"Thank you, Carly," Lanell said to her new sister-in-law. She started to say more, but paused, studying Carly's face more closely. She had become a dear friend and colleague, and with the change in relationship had come the ability to read her moods. Her gaiety sounded forced, her expression faintly troubled. "Are you still worried about your friend Heidi?" Lanell asked softly.

Carly nodded. "She's having trouble finding a decent job with an unjustified forced termination on her record. I hate seeing her depressed."

"Maybe it's time for her to start her own business. From what you've told me, she's qualified and experienced enough."

Carly's expression brightened. "I'll float that idea to her. Maybe I'll even check out possible rental quarters and start-up financing first. Thanks."

A few minutes later, Carly leaned over and spoke past Lanell to Connor. "Okay, you can take your bride and run now, Big Brother." Her tone gentled. "Take care of her as well as you've always taken care of me."

He gave her a nose-wrinkling look of agreement. Then he stood and pulled Lanell to her feet, entwining his fingers with hers. "Let's go," he said, his lazy grin warming her to her toes.

People headed for the exit ahead of them, apparently having received a signal from Carly. They lined each side of the porch and steps, throwing rice and calling well wishes as Connor led Lanell through the doorway and outside.

Once inside Connor's SUV, he turned and pulled

her into his arms. "I love you, and I can't wait to start our life together and see what God has in store for us."

"And I love you," she said, her heart swelling until she thought it would burst.

He kissed her and then started the motor. "Let's skip town, Mrs. Prescott."

ROMANCE BOOKS
by Helen

Ozark Sweetheart
Ozark Reunion
Ozark Wedding

Bandit Bride
Prairie Bride

Bootheel Bride
Bootheel Bachelor
Bootheel Betrothal

Show Me Love
Heartland Illusions
Mozark Vision
Missouri Catch

Paige's Proposal
Brooke's Bargain
Haley's Hero
Kelsey's Keeper

NOVELLAS
Hawthorn Hope
Tree of Hope
River Town Romance
(2 in 1, Hawthorn Hope
& Tree of Hope)

Pasque Plight
Black-Eyed Susan's
Secret
Love Blooms (2 in 1,
Pasque Plight & Black-
Eyed Susan's Secret)

Shamrock Ruby
Dream Team
Mother Road Matches
(2 in 1, Shamrock Ruby
& Dream Team)

Secrets in the Park
Gift Bride (Sequel to
Dodge City Duos)

MYSTERY BOOKS
by Helen
Educated in Murder
Preyed in Murder
Coached in Murder
Rivaled in Murder

www.ingramcontent.com/pod-product-compliance
Lightning Source LLC
Chambersburg PA
CBHW032209170626
46808CB00006B/2402

* 9 7 8 1 9 4 6 9 3 9 7 1 5 *